TRAPPED!

Running like a frightened hare, Andrew fled down a dark street. Behind him he heard the pounding of heavy boots. Then he ran into something solid but yielding and staggered back.

"Ow! Easy, duck," said a hoarse voice—a woman's voice. "Someone after you?"

"It's not the police," Andrew said. "It's . . ."

Without warning he was knocked to the floor . . .

"A first-rate mystery."
>   —*Booklist* (A Notable Children's Book)

"Great mystery!"
>   —*The Reading Teacher* (IRA)

"I enjoyed it heartily."
>   —Christopher Lehmann-Haupt,
>   *The New York Times*

The Case of the
Baker Street Irregular

A Sherlock Holmes Story

Robert Newman

This low-priced Bantam Book
has been completely reset in a type face
designed for easy reading, and was printed
from new plates. It contains the complete
text of the original hard-cover edition.
NOT ONE WORD HAS BEEN OMITTED.

RL 5, IL 5-up

THE CASE OF THE BAKER STREET IRREGULAR
A Bantam Book/published by arrangement with
Atheneum Publishers

PRINTING HISTORY
Atheneum edition published March 1978
6 printings through May 1980
A Selection of The Literary Guild December 1977
The use of the characters created by Arthur Conan Doyle
is by permission of the copyright owners.
Bantam edition/January 1981

Bantam Books are published by Bantam Books, Inc. Its trademark, consisting of the words "Bantam Books" and the por-
trayal of a bantam, is Registered in U.S. Patent and Trademark
Office and in other countries. Marca Registrada. Bantam
Books, Inc., 666 Fifth Avenue, New York, New York 10103.

PRINTED IN THE UNITED STATES OF AMERICA

0 9 8 7 6 5 4 3 2 1

For Dorothy Olding
with love.

Contents

The Case of the
Baker Street Irregular

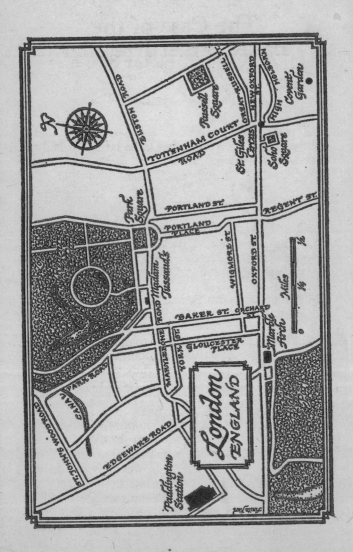

1

A Walk on Baker Street

Andrew had expected London to be large. He had not expected it to be frightening. But as the green fields gave way to seemingly endless rows of small, mean houses he began to feel uneasy. And when the train, moving more slowly, entered the dim vastness of the station and even the sky disappeared, his uneasiness increased. Of course it was all new and strange, but there was more to it than that. He was not sure exactly what it was that he found so disturbing, but he felt more lost and vulnerable than he had at any time during the past months.

The train stopped with a clash of buffers.

"Paddington!" shouted the guard.

Mr. Dennison took his portmanteau down from the net rack overhead, and Andrew took down his smaller bag. Mr. Dennison opened the door, and they stepped out on to the platform. The grimy roof arched over them, holding in and accentuating the noise: the babble of voices, clatter of baggage barrows and the hiss of steam from the still panting engine.

A porter eyed them hopefully, but Mr. Dennison ignored him and led the way toward the exit. For some reason Andrew found this reassuring. He might not like Mr. Dennison, but as long as he was with him he was safe. They surrendered their tickets at the barrier and went out to the street. Several four-wheelers—which Andrew knew were called growlers—and a few of the more graceful two-wheeled hansoms were lined up there. Andrew hoped they would take a hansom. He had never seen one before, much less ridden in one. But Mr. Dennison led the way to one of the growlers and said, "How much to twenty-four York Street?"

The cabby looked at him shrewdly—at his worn travelling ulster, his portmanteau and Andrew's old-fashioned bag—and said, "That'd be one and six, sir."

"It should be a bob."

The cabby shrugged.

"All right, guv'ner. Make it that."

They handed up their luggage and got in. The cabby flicked his whip, clucked to the bony horse, and they moved off into the traffic—the drays, hansoms, and brightly-colored, horse-drawn omnibuses—that clattered and rumbled by under the iron standards of the gaslights.

Sitting close to one of the windows, Andrew looked out at the buildings, the shops and the people—more people than he had ever seen before in his life: beggars, crossing sweepers with their brooms, ragged boys with shoeshine boxes, women wrapped in shawls, and anonymous men wearing caps or billycock hats. He was tired and hungry—it had been a long trip from Penzance—and he found the drab streets near the station depressing, but that was not what made him anxious, for he felt no better when they turned into a tree-shaded avenue that was lined with imposing houses. Then suddenly the reason for it came to him. London frightened him because it was what he had always sensed the world to be: not only huge and full of strangers, but strange in itself, impossible to comprehend. In Gorlyn, because it was so familiar and because he had not looked beneath the surface, the strangeness was hidden. Here it was open and naked, surrounding him.

It took about ten minutes to get to York Street, which was quiet and residential. The growler stopped in front of a four-story brick house and they got out. The cabby lifted down their bags and Mr. Dennison paid him. The cabby looked at the coins in his hand, at Mr. Dennison, then said dryly, "Thanks, guv'ner," and drove off.

It was clear that if Mr. Dennison had tipped him at all, it was a very small tip, which did not surprise Andrew. He was used to living modestly—his Aunt Agnes had been very careful about money—but she had been wildly extravagant compared to Mr. Dennison. That was why he had been so puzzled when the schoolmaster had said he was taking him to London. On the other hand, Mr. Dennison had done several surprising things during the past six months, the most astonishing of which had been to take Andrew in to live with him after Aunt Agnes had died.

A plump, pleasant looking woman opened the door almost immediately after Mr. Dennison tugged at the bell pull.

"Mrs. Gurney?" he asked. And when she nodded, "I'm Herbert Dennison and this is my ward, Andrew Craigie."

"It's nice to meet you, sir. I've been expecting you."

"I take it that you received my letter, then."

"I did. Your room is ready. Will you come this way?"

Picking up their bags, Andrew and Mr. Dennison followed her in and up a flight of stairs. She opened the door to a large room that faced York Street. After the simplicity of the cottage in Gorlyn, it seemed lavishly furnished to Andrew. For there was not only a bed, a couch, a table, desk and several arm chairs in it, but the floor was carpeted.

"You said your young friend would not mind sleeping on a couch," said Mrs. Gurney as Mr. Dennison looked around.

"I'm sure he won't. This seems quite satisfactory."

"Then, as I wrote you, my terms are a week paid in advance."

"Oh, yes. Yes, of course." And with barely noticeable reluctance he gave her a pound note and some change.

3

"Thank you, sir. Now would you like tea?"

"We would indeed." Then as a bell sounded outside, "Is that the muffin man?"

"It should be." She went to the window where Andrew was watching a man in a long apron coming up the street carrying a basket covered with green baize and ringing a brass bell. "Yes, it is. Would you like muffins with your tea?"

"If it's no trouble. They're one of the many things I've been missing since I left London."

"Then you shall have them. I'll be up shortly."

Mr. Dennison took out his wallet again after she left and counted the money in it. Then, catching Andrew's eye, he forced a smile.

"Sorry, Andrew," he said in his meticulous drawl. "I'm afraid I've been rather neglecting you. What do you think of our metropolis?"

"I don't really know, sir. I haven't seen very much of it so far."

"That's true. And I think we should do something about that. We'll go out for a bit of a walk later on."

There was cake as well as toasted muffins for tea, and though Mr. Dennison seemed as lost in his own thoughts as he had been during their journey from Cornwall—as he had been, in fact, for several weeks before it—he ate with as good an appetite as Andrew. When they were finished, he led the way out of the house and up York Street to a wide thoroughfare which, according to a street sign, was Baker Street.

It must have been close to six o'clock by now, but traffic was still heavy and the sidewalk was crowded with people, mostly well dressed but with a scattering of ragged urchins among them, who either walked briskly or sauntered, looking in the shop windows.

Mr. Dennison turned left. His pale face was suddenly eager and intent, and he walked quickly, hardly aware it seemed, that Andrew was with him. As they passed a sedate brick and stone house in the middle of the block, the door opened and a pair of striking looking men came out. One was tall and lean with a hawklike face

4

and piercing grey eyes. The other was shorter and more heavily built with a clipped military mustache and a face like an amiable bulldog. They both wore frock coats and silk hats and they were apparently in a hurry. The tall, hawkfaced man put two fingers to his lips, whistled shrilly, and a hansom cut in sharply in front of a bright green omnibus and drew up at the curb. Ignoring the fury of the omnibus driver, the cabby pulled the lever that opened the half door, the two men got in, and the hansom was off, rocking and swaying but moving swiftly through the traffic.

Mr. Dennison had gone ahead as Andrew paused to watch this. But when Andrew hurried to catch up with him, he found that Mr. Dennison had stopped also and was standing in front of a door with a brass plaque beside it that read: STROUD AND DEXTER, SOLICITORS. He glanced at this, at the windows above, then, apparently remembering Andrew, he turned and said, "Oh, there you are. What would you like to do now?"

"I don't know, sir. You said we'd go out for a walk."

"I also said I'd show you a bit of London. Well, let's see. This is Marylebone Road here. And over there," pointing to an imposing brick building across the road to the right, "is Madame Tussaud's. You've heard of that, haven't you?"

"No, sir. I'm afraid I haven't."

"Oh? Well, it's a famous museum, filled with full-sized wax figures of ancient and modern notables. Very educational. You'd probably be particularly interested in the Chamber of Horrors that contains, not only the effigies of notorious criminals, but the guillotine that decapitated Louis the Sixteenth and Marie Antoinette. We'll have to go there sometime."

"Yes, sir."

"Up ahead is Regent's Park. We'll have to go there also, visit the Zoological Gardens. Now let's go the other way."

They turned and walked back down Baker Street, past York Street, past a large and handsome square to Oxford Street, which was even wider and busier than

Baker Street. During this time Mr. Dennison had not said another word to Andrew. But now, turning to him, he said, "I think that's enough for today. There are some things I must do. You can find your way back to Mrs. Gurney's, can't you?"

"I think so, sir."

"Good. Tell her I won't be there for supper, probably not until quite late. I'll see you in the morning."

"Yes, sir."

Andrew watched him stride off, then turned and went back up Baker Street. He walked more slowly this time, marvelling at the number of shops and their variety; a furrier, a photographer, a shop that sold china and glass, and something called the Baker Street Bazaar that seemed to sell almost everything. Just before he reached York Street a shop on the other side of Baker Street caught his eye and he crossed over to it, dodging the hansoms, four-wheelers and omnibuses.

The sign over the door said JONATHAN WALKER, IMPORTS AND EXPORTS, and behind the large window was a strange and wonderful collection of objects: oriental rugs and curious curved swords, brassware and pewter, glass vases and figures, scarabs, cameos and musical instruments. Andrew stood there for some time, wondering where the various things came from, then crossed back again, went up York Street and pulled at the bell next to the door of Number Twenty-four.

He heard it jangle somewhere in the distance, and after a moment Mrs. Gurney opened the door.

"Oh, it's you," she said. "I didn't realize you'd gone out. Are you alone?"

"Yes, Mrs. Gurney. Mr. Dennison said to tell you he wouldn't be back for supper."

"Ah. And when would you like yours? I expect rather soon."

"It doesn't matter."

"Of course it matters. Growing boys are always hungry. At least mine always were. Well, if you'll go up, I'll be along shortly."

Andrew went up to the room, and a few minutes later Mrs. Gurney entered carrying a tray, which she put down on the table.

"I hope you like veal and ham pie," she said.

"Yes, I do."

"And bread pudding?"

"Yes."

"Well, sit down and eat. I'll make up the couch for you in the meantime."

While Andrew was eating, she took linen, a pillow, and a blanket from a large wardrobe.

"Mr. Dennison said your name was Craigie."

"Yes. Andrew Craigie."

"That would be Scottish, wouldn't it?"

"Yes."

"You don't sound like a Scot."

"I don't suppose I do. I've lived in Cornwall all my life."

"Where in Cornwall?"

"Gorlyn. It's a small village near Penzance."

"Ah, yes. That was the address on the letter Mr. Dennison wrote me. A pleasant gentleman, he seems. Here on business, is he?"

"Yes. At least, I believe so."

"What did he mean when he said you were his ward?"

"I think he meant that he's been taking care of me. I've been living with him ever since my aunt died."

"Your aunt? What about your parents?"

"My father's dead also. And my mother's been away for some time."

"I see. I'm sorry. Is Mr. Dennison a relative then?"

"No. He was one of the masters at school. He taught me there at first and then later at home."

"Ah. A tutor, like."

"Yes, I suppose so."

"I thought he talked like a university man. Well, it's all very interesting. I wasn't trying to pry, you understand, but I do like to know something about my roomers."

"Yes, of course."

She had finished making up the couch by now.

"It's getting a bit dim in here. Wouldn't you like some light?"

"Yes, thank you. I was wondering about that, but I didn't see any candles or lamps."

Mrs. Gurney smiled. "We're a bit more up to date than that. We have gas here."

She took a box of matches from the night table, turned a knob on a brass wall fixture over it, struck a match, and held it up under the glass shade. The room was immediately filled with soft yellow light.

"There you are. When you're ready for bed just turn this."

"Yes, Mrs. Gurney. Thank you. And thank you for supper."

"You're welcome. I'll see you in the morning. Good night."

"Good night, Mrs. Gurney."

She left, taking the tray, and Andrew went over to the window. He had no idea what time it was, but it was starting to get dark. There was a street light almost opposite him, and he was wondering who lit it and how when an elderly man came up the street carrying a pole with a hook and a brass cylinder at one end. He raised the pole, pulled something just under the glass globe of the light with the hook, and held the brass cylinder there for a moment. There must have been a lit wick inside, for the light flared even more brightly than the one in the room.

Andrew watched the lamplighter until he turned the corner and disappeared. Then, suddenly aware of how tired he was, he undressed, turned off the light and got in between the sheets on the couch.

Though he was tired, he was not sleepy and he lay there with his eyes wide open, staring into the darkness. Mrs. Gurney's questions had called up the ones he had been asking himself recently. Why had Mr. Dennison spent so much time with Aunt Agnes before she died? Why had he wanted Andrew to come live with him afterward when he didn't like Andrew any more than Andrew liked him? And why had he brought Andrew to London with him?

He had no better answer for these than he had for the other questions he had asked himself—and Aunt Agnes—for as long as he could remember.

Who was his father? Was he really dead? And where was his mother? If she really loved him, as Agnes had always insisted she did, why had it been years since she had come to see him? And if, as Agnes had claimed, she was far, far away, why didn't she write to him?

Agnes' face, gaunt and drawn as it had been near the end of her illness, came back to him. She had loved him as much as he had loved her—he knew that without any question—even though, for reasons he could never understand, she had been reluctant to show it. But she was gone now, and he had no one—no one in the world. No. That wasn't true. There was Jack Trefethen.

Andrew saw him again, looking as he had when Andrew went to say goodbye to him: big and bearded, wearing his leather apron and standing next to the anvil with his hammer in his hand. He had not been to Oxford like Mr. Dennison and, like most Cornishmen, he spoke little. But Andrew had learned more from him—and valued what he had learned more highly—than anything he had learned from Dennison.

The old familiar emotions—anxiety and anger, loneliness and resentment—began their complex assault on him and, gritting his teeth, he fought them off. He would forget his questions: would not think of what had happened to him, what he longed for and had been denied, not now. Even Trefethen—who would not tolerate softness or anything that resembled self-pity—could ask no more of him than that. Perhaps, when they got back to Gorlyn, he could persuade Mr. Dennison to let him go live with Trefethen. If he couldn't—or if the blacksmith didn't want him—at least he could talk to him, which was more than he could do with Mr. Dennison.

A horse's hoofs clopped hollowly by. Somewhere up the street a door opened and closed. From even farther

9

away, probably Baker Street, he could hear the rumble of traffic. It seemed to become fainter and fainter, and finally he no longer heard it.

2

Screamer

Mr. Dennison finished his tea, pushed back his chair and stood up.

"Well, I'm off," he said.

When Andrew finally fell asleep the night before, he had slept so soundly that he had not heard Mr. Dennison return. And when he woke in the morning Mr. Dennison was already up, shaving, and then dressing with particular care. As usual, he had said nothing during breakfast except to tell Andrew that he would be gone for most of the day.

"Would it be all right if I went out too, sir?" asked Andrew.

"What? Where do you want to go?"

"No place in particular. I just thought I'd walk around a little."

Mr. Dennison looked at him thoughtfully.

"I can think of no reason why you shouldn't. Very well. Tell Mrs. Gurney I won't be here for lunch."

"Yes, sir."

They went down the stairs together, and Andrew knocked at Mrs. Gurney's door and gave her Mr. Dennison's message. When he left the house, Mr. Dennison was still in sight, walking toward Baker Street. Andrew walked that way too. Reaching the corner, Mr. Dennison hesitated, looked at his watch, then turned left as he had the night before and walked north. When Andrew turned the corner, he was only a short distance behind Mr. Dennison, who was walking more briskly now, swinging his umbrella. It was still early, and though several shop assistants were out, opening shutters and sweeping the sidewalk, there were very few pedestrians. This may have been why Andrew noticed the tall gentleman with the neatly trimmed beard who was coming toward them. He was elegantly dressed in a morning coat and a silk hat. He glanced at Mr. Dennison, then looked at him again more sharply. Mr. Dennison did not seem to be aware of this and walked on past him. The bearded man stopped and stared after him. A grey-haired and ragged beggar, hat in hand, stood near the corner. He said something to the bearded man, who took out a coin, dropped it in the hat, then crossed Baker Street and entered Jonathan Walker's, the shop that had so interested Andrew the night before.

When Andrew turned back, looking for Mr. Dennison, he was gone. He stood there for a moment, thinking. Ahead of him he saw the green of Regent's Park, and he decided he would go there, possibly to the Zoological Gardens. As he started toward it, three disreputable looking boys of about his own age and a girl who was somewhat younger came hurrying down the street. One of the boys rang the bell next to the door of a brick and stone house, the door opened and the boys went in, leaving the girl outside.

Andrew studied her as he approached. She was about eleven or twelve, pale and quite thin, with large grey eyes and long straight hair. Though her dress was faded and seemed a little large for her it was clean and freshly ironed.

"Got your eye full?" she asked aggressively.

"I beg your pardon?"

"Who you staring at?"

"I'm sorry. I didn't realize I was."

"Well, you were. I've as much right to be here as anyone."

"Of course you have."

She relaxed a little.

"You do talk funny."

He had been thinking the same thing about her, for her speech was flat and rather nasal and she said "Oo"

12

for "who", droping her h's. But he saw no point in saying so.

"Funny how?"

"Almost like a toff. But you don't look like one. You're not from around here, are you?"

"No. I'm from Cornwall."

"Where's that?"

"South and west as far as you can go."

Her large eyes widened.

"Near the sea?"

"Yes."

"I've never seen the sea."

"Never?"

"No."

"Well, I've never seen London before."

"But you're seeing it now."

"Well, yes."

"What's your name?"

"Andrew. What's yours?"

"Screamer."

"Screamer?"

"That's what they call me. It's not my real name. That's Sara. Sara Wiggins."

"I think I like Sara better."

"I don't mind Screamer. I'm used to it. Where you off to?"

"Regent's Park. The Zoological Gardens."

"What's that?"

"Where the animals are."

"Animals?"

"Yes. Lions and tigers and elephants. Haven't you ever been there?"

"No."

"Why not?"

Screamer shrugged. Andrew was fairly sure the reason was that she didn't know it existed, but she couldn't bring herself to say so. Instead she dropped her eyes.

Because he had asked the wrong question, their conversation had suddenly come to an end. But Andrew was reluctant to leave. She was the first person anywhere near his own age that he had talked to in some time—not just since he had come to London but even before that. For when, much against his will, he had left the local school to study with Mr. Dennison, he had found himself cut off from all his former friends. From then on they had either avoided him or treated him with outright hostility.

As Andrew hesitated, the house door slammed open and the three boys came out. The tallest, a boy in a ragged coat whose closely cut hair stood up in spikes, looked at Andrew and then at Screamer.

"Who's that?" he asked.

"Andrew," said Screamer. "This is my brother, Sam. And Alf and Bert."

The three boys looked Andrew up and down and then ignored him.

"We're off," said Sam to Screamer. "We've got a job to do for Mr. Holmes. You cut along home."

"No," said Screamer.

"What do you mean, no?"

"I mean I don't want to go home and I'm not going."

Sam scowled. "Now look, Screamer," he began, moving toward her threateningly.

Screamer looked at him calmly, steadily, and made an ominous noise deep in her throat.

"Don't!" said Sam, drawing back. "Not here!" Then, giving up, "All right. Don't go, then. I'll see you later." And he and his two companions went running off.

Andrew looked at her with respect as well as interest.

"Who's Mr. Holmes?" he asked.

"Mr. Sherlock Holmes."

"You say that as if I should know who he is."

"Well, you should. He's the most famous detective in London. Maybe in the world."

"You mean he's with the police?"

"No, no. He doesn't have nothing to do with the police. He doesn't even like them. He's a private detective."

"Oh. And your brother works for him?"

14

"Yes. Him and Alf and Bert and one or two others. Not all the time but when he needs something special done. He calls them the Baker Street Irregulars."

"I see." Then, making up his mind, "Would you like to come to the zoo with me?"

Her eyes widened. "Do you mean it?"

"Of course."

"Then . . . yes, I would."

"Come on, then."

They went up Baker Street, crossed Marylebone Road and entered the park, walking past a lake and carefully tended gardens to the south entrance of the zoo. Andrew was a little disconcerted to find that there was an admission charge, but he had almost five shillings, money he had saved from what Trefethen had given him for helping out at the forge, and he did not want to disappoint Screamer. So, even though she protested, he paid, and they went in and entered the first building to their left.

"Coo!" said Screamer, staring. "What are those?"

"Different kinds of deer," said Andrew. "Those are red deer. That's a moose and that's an elk."

"You've been here before, then?"

"No."

"Then how do you know?"

"Because the signs tell you what they are." He glanced at her. "Can't you read?"

She looked away. "I know the letters, but I can't always put them together."

"Of course you can. What does that say?"

"B-i-son."

"That's right. Bison. They're also called buffaloes."

"Oh." She stared at the shaggy beasts. "They're awful big."

"Yes, they are. But the American Indians used to hunt them. They'd chase them on horseback and shoot them with bows and arrows."

"How do you know that?"

"I read about it."

"You do know a lot, don't you?"

"Not really." But he was pleased, enjoying himself thoroughly. It was fun just to be there, seeing animals he had only read about before. But to be there with someone who listened so intently to everything he said made it even more memorable. Still he continued to insist that Screamer try to read the signs, helping her when she had difficulty.

When they stood in front of the open enclosure behind the Lion House and a large, maned male woke from his morning nap and came close to the bars to blink at them, Screamer took his hand and, for most of the rest of the morning, she held on to it.

Screamer was so enchanted by the seals and penguins that shared a pool—the seals diving, swimming, and barking and the penguins strutting about like little men in dress clothes—that he had difficulty in getting her to go on. By the time they had looked at the giraffes, the hippopotami and the elephants, it was long past noon.

"Are you hungry?" asked Andrew.

"Fair starved."

"So am I. Let's get something to eat."

He started toward a refreshment stand, but Screamer said, "Wait. You paid to get us in. I'll pay for lunch."

"Have you got any money?"

"No, but I'll get some. I'll do a lucifer drop."

"A what?"

"A lucifer drop. Mum and Sam say it's mumping and I shouldn't do it, but what they don't know won't hurt 'em. Wait here."

"But . . ."

"I said, wait here. It's no good if I'm not alone."

She looked around, then walked back to the Elephant House. There she took a box of matches out of her pocket, partially opened it and, standing next to the doorway, said in a small voice, "Lucifers, tuppence a box. Lucifers."

Andrew watched, puzzled. People coming out of the Elephant House or pushing their way in paid no attention to her, but that didn't seem to disturb Screamer. A well-dressed, elderly man accompanied by a young

16

woman and two small boys came out, and Screamer edged forward. The man brushed against her, and the box fell to the ground, spilling most of the matches. Screamer looked down at them and burst into tears.

"What is it? What's wrong?" asked the elderly man.

"Can't you see what you done?" said a beefy man in a cap. "You knocked the blooming matches out of 'er 'and."

"Oh. I am sorry, my dear," said the elderly man. "I didn't see you. Here." And he gave her a coin.

"A tanner!" said the man with the cap scornfully. "Don't beggar yourself!"

"Are you presuming to tell me how much to give her?" said the elderly man, drawing himself up.

"I ain't presuming nothing," said the man with the cap. "Here y'are, ducky. Here's a bob."

"Oh, thank you, sir," said Screamer.

"Father, I really do think . . ." said the young woman.

"Oh, very well," said the elderly man. "Here." And he gave Screamer another coin.

"Thank you, sir. Thank you kindly."

Wiping her eyes with her sleeve, she bent down and began picking up the matches.

A small crowd had gathered.

"Poor child," said a matronly looking woman.

"Probably hasn't had a decent meal in days," said another. "Here, pet."

Three or four more people pressed money on Screamer, then went on or into the Elephant House. Screamer finished picking up the matches, then returned to Andrew.

"Three and six," she said. "That should do it." Then as Andrew looked at her, "Why are you looking at me that way? I didn't ask for nothing, did I?"

"No."

"Then what's wrong with it?"

"Nothing."

"All right, then. Let's eat."

They went over to the refreshment stand and she

paid for sandwiches, buns and tea for the two of them.

They left the zoo late in the afternoon, tired by all the walking they had done and bemused by all that they had seen. They sat for a while on the grass near the lake watching the rowers, most of whom, Andrew thought, did not handle their boats particularly well. When they finally got up, Screamer said, "Let's go this way," and led him out through Park Square and along Portland Place.

"Where are we going?" he asked.

"No place. I just like walking through here. There ain't no shops to look at like on Baker Street, but it's even fancier."

"It is nice," said Andrew, looking at the elegant facades of the houses that lined the street. Then, pointing to an imposing stone building, "What's that?"

"A hotel. The Hotel Langham. I once saw a duchess going in there."

"How'd you know it was a duchess?"

"How do you think? I asked."

That was logical. Though Screamer had been subdued, even a little uncertain, when they had first gone into the zoo, later on, and especially when they were back in the streets that were so familiar to her, she was completely sure of herself.

As they approached the hotel a growler, piled high with luggage, drew up. The uniformed attendant seemed to be expecting it, for when he had glanced inside, he touched his hat and beckoned. Three page boys came hurrying out of the hotel and lined up beside him. Then he opened the cab door, and the most beautiful lady Andrew had even seen stepped out.

Her hair was tawny, her skin very white and her eyes were a startling cornflower blue. She wore a large hat with ostrich feathers on it and a long traveling cape. She was very gay, smiling at the cabby as she paid him and chatting with the commissionaire while the luggage was handed down. Several people had stopped and were watching, and Screamer and Andrew joined them.

"Who is she?" asked Andrew as the lady followed the commissionaire into the hotel.

"I dunno," said Screamer. "I'll find out."

She worked her way through the crowd, talked to one of the page boys who was carrying the luggage into the hotel, then came back again.

"Her name's Verna Tillet and she's an actress," she said. "She's been in America and she's going to be opening at the Adelphi next week."

Andrew nodded. He had never seen either an actress or a duchess before, but he would much rather see the former than the latter, especially since she looked just the way he had imagined an actress would look.

"It's getting late and I should be getting back," he said. "Are we far from York Street?"

"No. This way."

Screamer led him through quiet, tree-shaded residential streets where maids in caps and white aprons were drawing the blinds of elegant houses. They reached Baker Street and were just starting north when Screamer paused.

"What is it?" asked Andrew.

"There's Alf and Bert."

Glancing up the street, Andrew saw the two boys who had been with Screamer's brother standing in front of number 221B. The door opened, and Sam came out. He gave his two friends a thumbs up sign, and they talked for a moment, their heads together. Then Sam saw Screamer and he came toward them.

"I was just going to start looking for you," he said. "Where you been?"

"Oh, places. The zoo. How'd you do?"

"All right. Mr. Holmes wanted us to find someone for him. It took us all day and we had to go clean to Bermondsey to do it, but we did."

"A criminal?"

"I've told you before, when you work for Mr. Holmes you don't ask questions." As before, he ignored Andrew. "Mum'll be home soon. Come on."

"Half a tick," said Screamer. "I want to say goodbye to Andrew and . . ."

"I said, come on!" said Sam and taking her by the arm, he hurried her off.

Andrew watched them go, suddenly feeling very much alone. He had felt a twinge of jealousy when he saw Sam talking to his two friends. It must, he had felt, be pretty exciting to be a Baker Street Irregular and work with a famous detective, and he couldn't help wondering who they had had to find and why. As for Screamer, there had been things he had wanted to say to her too—or rather ask her. For though she was younger than he was and rather odd, he had enjoyed being with her and would have liked to see her again. But she had told him nothing about herself, and he had no idea where she lived.

He started home slowly. It must have been well after tea time, for though it was still light the streets were almost deserted. He turned into York Street and there, some distance ahead of him, he saw Mr. Dennison. He was walking quickly but there was no mistaking him even from the back.

Andrew was too tired to hurry, and besides—though it was unlikely that Mr. Dennison would question him—he wasn't ready yet to talk about Screamer or what he had done all day. So he stepped behind a stoop, intending to wait until after Mr. Dennison had gone into Mrs. Gurney's before he went in himself.

But just as Mr. Dennison reached for the bell pull, a growler drew up and a man got out. At the same time the cabby climbed down from the box, and they both approached Mr. Dennison. Andrew was too far away to hear what they said to him, but Mr. Dennison seemed to shrink back. Then the man had him by the arm and was leading him to the curb. The two men got into the growler, the cabby climbed back into the box, cracked his whip and the horse broke into a trot. As the growler clattered past, Andrew saw that the cabby, a heavyset man with a crooked, broken nose, was grinning.

Puzzled and a little uneasy, Andrew watched the

four-wheeler turn the corner and disappear. Who was the man who had spoken to Mr. Dennison? Was he a friend? From the way the schoolmaster had acted, Andrew didn't think so. On the other hand, Mr. Dennison had come to London on business. Perhaps the stranger was the man he had come to see and they had not met before this. Yes, that must be it. If it wasn't, how would the man know where Mr. Dennison was staying? In any case, there was nothing he could do about it until Mr. Dennison returned. Then, though he never discussed his affairs with Andrew, he might explain.

"Oh, there you are," said Mrs. Gurney when he opened the door. "I was starting to worry about you. Where's Mr. Dennison?"

"He just went off somewhere."

"Oh? Will he be here for supper?"

"I'm afraid I don't know."

"Well, I like to be accommodating," she said, frowning, "but I must say this is a little too much. I mean, if he's not going to be here, don't you think I should be told?"

"Yes, of course. But I'm not sure he knew himself. It all happened very suddenly."

"Sudden or not, it's not right. But it's not your fault. What I'll do is give you your supper now and keep something for him. If he's not too late, he can have it when he gets home."

"Fine, Mrs. Gurney."

He went up to the room, ate his supper and then stretched out on the couch. After all the walking he had done, he was even more tired than he had been the day before, but he was determined not to go to sleep until Mr. Dennison returned. Fixing his eye on the gaslight, he began to think about everything that had happened that day; all the pleasant things like his meeting with Screamer and their visit to the zoo. But always in the background there was something that was not so pleasant. That was, in fact, very disturbing and that he kept pushing away and trying not to think about. Suppose the man in the growler, the man who had driven off with Mr. Dennison, wasn't a friend? Suppose he were an enemy or a criminal, and Mr. Dennison didn't come back? It was ridiculous, of course. Things like that couldn't happen in London. But if that's what had happened, what would become of him, Andrew? With no friends or money, where would he go? What would he do?

The Disturbance at
the Empire Club

Dr. Watson ran his eye over the back page of the news-paper, folded it and dropped it to the floor.

"So you found the paper rather dull today," said Holmes.

"Yes, I did," said Watson. Then he turned. Holmes, sitting at his desk and going through one of his scrap-books, had his back to him. "How did you know?"

"It usually takes you forty-three minutes to get through it. Today it only took you thirty-six." Holmes swung around. "If you're finished with it, may I have it?"

"Of course." Watson handed him the paper, watched as he opened it to an inside page, picked up his scissors and cut something out. "Did I miss something?"

"You may not have missed it, but apparently it didn't interest you. However it did interest me."

Watson got up and went over to the desk where Holmes was pasting the clipping into the scrapbook. It was captioned *Disturbance at the Empire Club*.

"Yes, I saw that. But when did you see it? You haven't read the paper yet."

"No. But you were holding it up when you ate your breakfast and it caught my eye."

"But why should it interest you? This fellow Lytell was obviously drunk."

"I doubt it. I've met him once or twice, and he didn't

strike me as someone who'd be drunk at four in the afternoon."

"But he must have been. According to the paper he not only created a disturbance by shouting and threatening several of the members but broke a large vase with his stick. And it wasn't even his own club."

"No. It was his father's, Lord Lowther's."

"But drunk or not, don't you still think his behavior was rather odd?"

"Very odd. That's why it interests me."

Watson shook his head. "I'm sorry, Holmes," he said. "I'm afraid . . ."

There was a discreet knock.

"Yes?" said Holmes.

"A gentleman to see you, Mr. Holmes," said the landlady, opening the door.

"Thank you, Mrs. Hudson. Would you show him in?"

"Yes, sir."

She stepped back and an intense and troubled-looking man in his early thirties came in. He was tall and fair and though his tweed suit was rather worn, it was very well cut.

"I hope you'll forgive me for dropping in this way, Mr. Holmes," he said. "I'm not sure if you remember me . . ."

"Of course I do," said Holmes. "We met at Sanderson's place, had an interesting discussion about Buxtehude's cantatas."

"You have a good memory."

"One of my many attributes. But, as it happens, Watson and I were just talking about you. My friend, Dr. John Watson. The Honorable Adam Lytell."

"How do you do, sir?" said Lytell. "But how did you happen to be talking about me?" Then, looking at the crumpled newspaper on the floor, "I see. You read about what happened at my father's club yesterday."

"We did."

"It was unfortunate that a reporter should happen to

be passing by at the time. But then you've probably guessed why I'm here."

"Possibly. But I'd rather you told me."

"Then . . . it's to consult you about that—what happened at the club—and what happened afterward."

"I'll wait inside, Holmes," said Watson, rising.

"Please stay, Dr. Watson," said Lytell. "I know that you have often been involved in Mr. Holmes' cases. And in this particular one it may be that it is you I should be consulting rather than he."

Watson glanced at Holmes, then sat down again.

"I must say that the story puzzled me a bit," said Holmes. "How much of it is true?"

"I suspect most of it."

"You suspect?"

"Yes. I'm not certain exactly what did happen."

"Had you been drinking?" asked Watson.

"No, doctor. I'm not a teetotaler—I like a glass of wine occasionally—but I'm not much of a drinking man."

"Perhaps you had better begin at the beginning," said Holmes. "When we last met, you had rooms in Bloomsbury."

"I still have."

"And where does your father live?"

"At the family estate at Norby Cross."

"And how good is your relationship with him?"

Lytell smiled grimly. "You do go to the heart of things, don't you? I would say that our relationship is, to say the least, strained."

"Will you tell us why?"

"Of course. While I was at Oxford I became interested in politics. Since my views were quite liberal and my father was a Tory, he was not exactly happy about it. But he believed that in time my political ideas would change."

"And did they?" asked Watson.

"On the contrary. When I came down to London, I decided that liberalism was not enough and I became a member of the Fabian Society. He liked that even less. But the last straw, as far as he was concerned, came a week ago when I became Secretary of the Society."

"How did he know this?" asked Holmes.

"I wrote and told him. I thought I should. He wrote back and said he must talk to me and suggested that we meet at his club."

"This was yesterday?"

"Yes. Since I've always admired him despite our differences, I had some misgivings about the meeting. I knew what he was going to say and I was uneasy about it. In fact, as I walked to the club, I had a real sense of foreboding."

"What do you mean?" asked Holmes.

"London suddenly seemed strange, menacing. The sky seemed darker than usual, the streets dirtier and noisier. I don't know how long it took me to get to the club . . ."

"Were you late?"

"I'm not sure. I have no clear recollection of anything that happened after that. I believe I asked for my father and was shown into the member's lounge, and it's my impression that as soon as he saw me, he began shouting at me and I shouted back. Then people began closing in on me, threatening me, and I have a feeling I fought them off. I have a vague memory of a policeman and a cab driver, and the next thing I knew I was lying on the bed in my rooms."

"What time was that?" asked Holmes.

"About nine in the evening."

"You said you had not been drinking. Where did you have lunch?"

"In my rooms. I was working on a pamphlet, and I had something sent in."

"Well, Watson?" said Holmes. "Any ideas?"

"Did you have any physical symptoms?" asked Watson. "Headache? Aches in your joints? Did you feel very hot?"

"You're thinking that he might have had a sudden high fever of some sort?" said Holmes.

Watson nodded. "I've known men to act as Mr. Lytell did when they were delirious."

"I had no symptoms that I recall. Just that overwhelming sense of anxiety. And I felt perfectly well when I woke up."

"And nothing like it has ever happened to you before?"

"No. My health generally is very good."

"Well, it's not really my field," said Watson. "And it might be wise to consult a specialist in nervous disorders . . ."

"You mean you think I may be losing my mind, going mad?"

"No, no. Nothing like that. Charcot in Paris has written of cases where patients of his developed similar symptoms when they were faced with extremely difficult emotional situations."

"Well, heaven knows it was a difficult situation," said Lytell. "But the one I face now is even more difficult."

"What is that?" asked Holmes.

"My father died last night."

"Died? How?"

"According to the message I received, from a heart attack. That he did die is bad enough. As I said, I liked and admired him. But if it was a heart attack, was I responsible?"

"You're thinking about the legal consequences?" said Holmes slowly. "About an inquest?"

"Legal consequences be damned!" said Lytell heatedly. "He was my father! How do you think I'll feel if it turns out that it was my fault? That's why I came here. Would you—the two of you—look into the matter for me?"

Holmes and Watson exchanged glances.

"Do you know who his doctor is?" asked Watson.

"Dr. Harvey Moore."

"Oh? I know him," said Watson. "But haven't you talked to him about it?"

"I tried to—last night when I heard the news—and again this morning. But he refused to see me."

"Strange," said Watson. "If you like, I'll go see him, talk to him."

"Now?"

"Yes," said Watson, rising. "You'll come too, Holmes?"

"Of course."

"I can't thank you enough," said Lytell. "May I come back again late this afternoon, say around five?"

"By all means," said Watson. "I should have some word for you by then."

"You know where to find Moore?" asked Holmes when Lytell had gone.

"His consulting rooms are on Harley Street," said Watson. "But he's usually at Bart's in the morning."

Holmes nodded and, familiar with his friend's silence and abstraction when he was thinking, Watson got his hat and followed Holmes down the stairs. Walking to the curb, Holmes waved to a hansom that was coming up Baker Street. It was only when it drew up that he saw the well-dressed man with the neatly trimmed beard who had apparently hailed it also.

"I beg your pardon," said Holmes. "I didn't realize . . ."

"It's quite all right," said the man. Then, looking at him more closely, "You're Mr. Sherlock Holmes, are you not?"

"I am."

"Then by all means take it. I'm certain that your business is more urgent than mine."

Watson knew that no one had a higher opinion of himself and his affairs than Holmes and so he was not surprised when his companion accepted this without protest.

"You're very kind," said Holmes, bowing to the bearded man. "Thank you."

He told the cabby to take them to Bart's; he and Watson got into the hansom, and it went rattling off.

They were both familiar with St. Bartholomew—in

fact they had first met there—and so they entered the hospital through the side door off Smithfield, climbed the stone staircase and, after Watson had made a few enquiries, paused at the entrance to a ward.

A florid, peppery looking man with grey hair was standing near one of the beds talking to some young doctors. He looked up, waved to Watson and, a moment later, came over to him.

"Haven't seen you in some time, Watson," he said. "How are you?"

"Fine, doctor. Do you know my friend, Mr. Sherlock Holmes?"

"No, I don't," said Moore, looking at him with interest. "Heard of you, of course. Here on one of your famous cases?"

"I'm not sure," said Holmes. "Actually I came here with Watson who wanted to talk to you about one of yours."

"Oh?" said Moore, turning back to Watson. "Which one was that?"

"Lord Lowther," said Watson. "I understand he was your patient."

"Patient and friend," said Moore. "I knew him, treated him, for more than twenty years. Tragic business, his death."

"Exactly what was the cause of death?"

"Why, heart attack."

"Is there any question about that?" asked Holmes.

"None whatsoever," said Moore emphatically. "I'm a member of his club too, and I was not only there with him when he died, but, as I said, I've taken care of him for more than twenty years. In fact, I was the one who first warned him of his condition."

"I see," said Holmes. "Exactly what time did he die?"

"A little before nine. Why?"

"His son, Adam, came to see us," said Watson, "and told us about the incident that had taken place in the afternoon. I assume you know about that."

"Indeed I do. Disgraceful!"

"Do you think that could have caused the attack?"

"No. That happened about four. Too long an interval."

"But still you refused to see him, talk to him," said Holmes.

"Of course I did. Don't like the fellow, didn't want to have anything to do with him."

"Why not?" asked Holmes.

"Because he's a Fabian!" snapped Moore. "Comes of a fine family, knew he'd inherit the title and pots of money some day and what does he do? Joins up with a group of wild-eyed crackpots who are calling for nationalization, socialism!"

"I gather his father felt the same way about it," said Holmes.

"Naturally."

"But you still don't think that Lytell's politics—or his behavior—had anything to do with Lord Lowther's death?"

"I told you I didn't. Lowther was furious at the way Adam behaved when he came to the club, but basically he liked him—liked his spirit—even though he didn't like his politics. Of course if it had been Lowther's other son, it might have been different."

"His other son?"

"The youngest—a real wrong 'un. Sent down from the university after a shocking scandal and shipped off to America. Terrible blow to Lowther. It was after that that he developed his heart condition. Anything else?"

"I don't believe so," said Watson, glancing at Holmes. "Thank you very much."

"Not at all," said Moore and nodding to Holmes, he went back into the ward.

"Well, Holmes?" said Watson.

"Interesting. At least now we know why Moore wouldn't talk to Lytell."

"And we also know that he wasn't responsible for his father's death. But I wonder what made him behave as he did at the club."

"That's even more interesting."

"In what way?"

"I'd rather not say at the moment. What about lunch? I could do with one of Simpson's chops."

They walked home after lunch and got to Baker Street at about three-thirty. As they turned into it from Oxford Street, a fire engine went past them, the horses trotting sedately.

"There seems to have been a fire," said Watson.

"Yes," said Holmes. "Not a very serious one."

"You think not?"

"I'm sure of it. The firemen didn't look as if they had had to exert themselves."

Accustomed as he was to such observations, Watson looked at Holmes skeptically but did not comment.

Mrs. Hudson was in the hall when they entered the house.

"Where was the fire, Mrs. Hudson?" asked Holmes.

"Oh, in a shop across the street. But it wasn't a bad one."

"It wasn't?" said Holmes with a glance at Watson.

"No, sir. I have a message for you. I was just about to take it upstairs." And she gave him a card.

Holmes thanked her, looked at the card, turned it over, then handed it to Watson. It was the business card of one Jonathan Walker who was an importer and exporter with a Baker Street address. On the back was written: *I would consider it a great favor if you would stop by at my shop. I have something of considerable importance to discuss with you. Very truly yours, Jonathan Walker.*

"Will you go?" asked Watson.

"Why not? It's just across the street."

"Would you like me to come with you?"

"If it would interest you, of course."

They crossed Baker Street and walked to the shop, which was near Crawford Street. As they went in, Holmes sniffed, and even Watson, whose senses were not as keen as his friend's, could detect the smell of smoke. The man in the rear of the shop looked familiar, and as he came toward them Watson recognized him as the well-dressed man with the beard who had so graciously surrendered the hansom to them that morning.

"Mr. Walker?" said Holmes.

"Yes, Mr. Holmes. It was very good of you to come."

"Not at all. I've been interested in your shop since you opened it, and I'm delighted to be able to repay your courtesy of this morning."

Walker bowed. "A happy accident. This, of course, is Dr. Watson."

"It is."

"I'm very pleased to meet you, sir. Would you care to look around, Mr. Holmes, or shall I come directly to the reason for my note?"

"Perhaps that would be best," said Holmes.

"Then let us go into my office. Sebastian," he said to an effete and rather languid looking young man, "see that we're not disturbed."

"Yes, Mr. Walker."

Holmes sniffed again as they entered the office.

"We saw an engine as we came home. The fire was here?"

"Yes, in my rear store room. I was out to lunch at the time, but fortunately Sebastian noticed it almost at once and there was not too much damage."

"Was that what you wished to talk to me about?"

"As it happens, I left the note for you on my way to lunch—before the fire. But there is a connection."

"Perhaps you had better begin at the beginning."

Pulling out chairs for them, Walker sat down at a large desk and looked gravely at Holmes.

"I doubt if there is anyone who understands the criminal mind better than you do. I am also convinced that you know more about the dark side of London than anyone else. Therefore, I would like to ask you a question. Do you believe it is possible that someone is trying to organize all crime here—in effect, become the ruler of the underworld?"

"It is certainly possible. It has happened before and will undoubtedly happen again. But why do you ask?"

"Because of certain things that have happened since I opened my shop here."

"I would like to hear about them."

"Very well. As you probably know, I opened the shop about six months ago. Before that I worked for an importer in Bristol, travelling and doing most of his buying. Shortly after I opened the shop, I began to feel that I was being watched. It may be that you know the feeling."

"I do."

"I kept my eyes open, tried to determine who was watching me but of course that was difficult. It could have been a beggar, a crossing sweeper or even someone who appeared to be a passerby. Then, a few weeks ago, I was approached and given what amounted to an ultimatum."

"By whom?"

"I don't know. I live in Kensington, and one night as I was returning home quite late, a four-wheeler drew up and someone in it addressed me by name."

"A man?"

"Yes. I started to go over to it but was told to keep my distance. The man said he gathered I was doing quite well in the shop and asked if I would like to do even better. When I asked how, he said he was in a position to supply me with a great deal of merchandise—merchandise of all sorts—if I would be willing to divide the profits with him. I asked him where the merchandise would come from, and he said that was no concern of mine. From which I gathered that the merchandise had been stolen."

"In other words, he was suggesting that you act as a fence."

"Exactly. Naturally I refused, and he said I was being very foolish. That if I would not accept his offer to help me make money, it was going to cost me money. That I was going to have to pay him a specific sum every month to keep my shop open."

"You mean pay him for protection."

"Yes. I told him I would do no such thing; and he

said he would give me a little time to think about it, and the growler drove off."

"You never saw the man?"

"No. The street was dark and he sat well back in the cab."

"What about the cabby and the cab number?"

"The cabby's hat was pulled down and a scarf covered his face. All I could see were his eyes. I tried to make out the cab number as it drove away, but it was covered, too."

Holmes nodded. "Those would be obvious precautions. What happened after that?"

"I was approached several times in the same way. Each time I told him I would not even consider his offer nor pay him to be able to conduct a legitimate business. And the last time, two nights ago, I told him that if he continued to harass me, I would go to the police. He laughed at this, said I was a stubborn fool and that it was time I was taught a lesson."

"And today you had a fire."

"Yes. As I said, I left the note for you before the fire, for I was determined to do something about what was happening. And now I am more determined than ever. The question is, what shall I do?"

"I would do what you told the man in the growler you would do," said Holmes. "Go to the police."

"That was what I planned to do originally," said Walker. "But then I thought . . . Could I possibly persuade you to take on the case, discover who the man in the growler was?"

Holmes shook his head. "He would not be the principal. He would just be the demander."

"But if you found out who he was, wouldn't that lead to the principal, the man who organized the conspiracy?"

"Possibly. But a great deal of evidence would have to be gathered, proving that similar demands had been made on other merchants. That there was, in fact, a conspiracy. And that is a job for the police. I think you should talk to Inspector Gregory about it. If you like, you can say that I suggested it."

"Very well," said Walker. "I won't pretend that I'm not disappointed. I think a great deal more of your capabilities than I do of theirs."

"In a case like this, you can have full confidence in the police. It's the kind of thing they handle very effectively."

"Then I'll go to see Inspector Gregory," said Walker. "And I thank you for your advice."

"Not at all," said Holmes, rising. "Let me know what he has to say about it."

"I'll certainly keep you informed," said Walker. He opened the door for Holmes and Watson. "You said before that you were interested in my shop. Do you have time to look around now?"

"I'm afraid not," said Holmes. "I'm expecting someone at our rooms and . . . Hello." He picked up a bound orchestral score. "I see you also sell music here."

"Some. I got this when I bought a musician's estate. Was there something in particular you wanted?"

"Yes. Bruch's Second Violin Concerto. I've been looking for it for some time."

"Have you tried Nordener in Covent Garden?"

"I've tried every music seller in London. Several of them have the first Concerto but no one has the Second."

"Well, I know a dealer in Paris who might have it. The next time I go over, I'll inquire about it for you."

"I would appreciate that. Thank you."

"Thank you for your patience and your counsel." And again Walker opened the door to let them out.

"Then you don't believe that someone is trying to organize London's underworld, Holmes?" asked Watson as they walked up the street.

"Someone is always trying to do so. I have no doubt that someone is trying to do so now."

"Then why wouldn't you take on the case?"

"Because," said Holmes testily, "as I told Walker, at the moment it is something the police are quite competent to handle. If a truly dangerous criminal leader should emerge—someone of real intelligence whose vision extends further than extortion and disposing of stolen goods—I shall be glad to match wits with him. Until then, I would rather concentrate on my own kind of case, the ones that are uncommon in some way and therefore intrigue me."

"Well, obviously you must do as you wish. But it's clear that Walker was disappointed. I must say that he's rather an unusual man for a shopkeeper."

"Very. An Oxford man, either a boxer or a cricketer, gets his clothes at Poole's and has his hair cut at Trumper's."

"Now really, Holmes!"

"I know. All elementary. Poole's clothes are unmistakable and so is the scent of Trumper's hair lotion. As for his athletic background, even you must have suspected that from the way he moves."

"I'm afraid I didn't—didn't notice any of the things you mentioned."

"Oh? After all this time I would have thought you'd be quite skillful at observing things and drawing deductions from them."

"I believe I am. For that is precisely what I do in medical matters," said Watson, nettled. "But I see no need to extend it to every aspect of my life—observe and make deductions about everyone I meet or see—as you seem to do."

"It's no longer intentional on my part. By now it's second nature."

"Is it? Then what can you tell me about that lad? It seems to me that I've seen him before."

They were at their door now, and Holmes glanced at the boy who was coming down the street, his eyes on them.

"So have I. Obviously it's more difficult to make deductions about someone his age than about a grown man."

"Obviously," said Watson dryly.

"All I can tell you is that he is from Cornwall where

he was friends with a blacksmith. That he is probably an orphan, staying at a rooming house rather than a hotel with someone who does not care for him very much."

"What?" Holmes had opened the door and, looking at the boy once more, Watson followed him inside. "I'm sorry, Holmes, but that's really too much!"

"Not at all. It has been unusually cloudy during these last few weeks but the boy is as tanned as a fisherman. The only place in England where he could have gotten so much sun is Cornwall. As for the blacksmith, if you had looked at him closely you would have seen several tiny burns on his clothes, the kind you get from sparks if you stand too close to a forge or anvil when iron is being hammered."

"And the rest?"

"If he had a father or mother or was in London with someone who really cared about him, they would have done something about the condition of his clothes—which were fairly good to begin with. They would also have seen to it that his hair was cut. As for the rooming house, his shoes badly needed brushing and polishing. If he had been staying at a hotel, he would have left them outside the door for the Boots to take care of."

"Well, of course, there's no way you can prove any of that."

"No way at all," said Holmes cheerfully. "Unless we ask him if we should see him again. But something else is troubling you."

"Yes. I've been thinking about what you said about Walker. If he's everything you claim, a gentleman, then why is he a shopkeeper?"

"A good question, Watson. A very good question."

4

Alone in London

Andrew watched the two men go into the house. When he had first seen them coming up the street, it had occurred to him that the taller of the two, the hawkfaced man with the penetrating eyes, might be Mr. Sherlock Holmes. And when they went into number 221B—the house Screamer's brother had come out of—he was convinced of it. But by that time it was too late.

Too late for what? Troubled and anxious though he was, he did not see how he could have gone up to the famous detective and asked for help or even advice.

Altogether it had been a bad and frightening day. When Andrew woke early that morning, Mr. Dennison was not there and his bed had not been slept in. He had dressed and, though Mrs. Gurney had been a little surprised when she brought up breakfast, she said she didn't see anything to be alarmed about. When gentlemen came to London, they often stayed out all night. Andrew might have been reassured if he had not felt she said this simply because she had other things on her mind—other lodgers to take care of—and did not want to be burdened with an additional problem. So he had not pursued the matter. However, he had not gone out but had stayed in the room all morning, trying to read one of the books he had brought with him, but spending most of his time looking out of the window.

By lunch time Mrs. Gurney had agreed that it was a little odd for Mr. Dennison to be staying away for so long without any word to Andrew. And when he finally told her about the strange way Mr. Dennison had gone off in the growler, she had looked grave.

"I don't think anything can be really wrong," she had said. "After all, this is London. But if he's not back by four o'clock or so, perhaps you should go to the police."

Dennison had not come back. And when Andrew had gone downstairs at a little after four and knocked on her door, it was clear that she was concerned. But it was also clear that she did not intend to become too involved in something that might be unpleasant. She told him that there was a police station on Marylebone Road, but she did not offer to go there with him. So he had walked over to Baker Street and started up it—and it was then that he had seen the man he was sure was Mr. Sherlock Holmes and his companion with the military mustache.

Andrew walked slowly on to Marylebone Road, then west to the police station. It was a square, solid, forbidding building, and he stood in front of it for several minutes. He had been awed by the few policemen he had seen since he came to London—their size, their helmets, and the measured way they walked—and he was sure that they would be even more frightening in official surroundings. Not only that, but he suspected that they, like Mrs. Gurney, would find it hard to believe that anything could happen to a grown man in London. He could imagine the exchange that would take place when he went in:

A sergeant looking down at him from the high desk. "Yes?"

"I want to report someone missing."

"Oh? And who is that?"

"Well, I suppose you could call him my guardian."

"You suppose?"

"Well, I've been living with him in Cornwall, and I came here to London with him three days ago."

"But he's not your legal guardian."

"No."

"How long has he been missing?"

"Since last night."

"I see. That's not very long, is it?"

As a matter of fact, it really wasn't very long. And if there was nothing unusual about someone staying out all night, as Mrs. Gurney had said, why shouldn't Mr. Dennison stay out a while longer, say until supper time? Perhaps he should wait until evening—or even until tomorrow morning before he talked to the police.

Knowing that he was temporizing, finding excuses for not doing something he found difficult, Andrew started back to the rooming house, this time by way of Gloucester Place. He rounded the corner into York Street, then paused. A growler was standing at the curb between him and Mrs. Gurney's. The cabby had his back to Andrew but there was something familiar about the set of his shoulders, the way his billycock hat was tipped forward. He did not seem to have discharged a fare, and he did not appear to be waiting for one: he was not looking at any of the buildings, he was looking straight ahead towards Baker Street. Suddenly, as if he sensed that someone was watching him, he turned around. It was the cabby with the crooked, broken nose who had driven Mr. Dennison off the night before.

At that moment Andrew knew—knew beyond any doubt—that the menace he had felt when Mr. Dennison got into the growler had not been imaginary. And he also knew that the cabby was now there for him.

With pretended casualness, he turned around and began to walk the other way. Behind him he heard the slap of reins, the creaking rasp of wheels and the sound of a horse's hoofs and, glancing back, he saw that the cabby had turned the growler and was coming after him. Crossing Gloucester Place, he turned south, then at the next corner went west again. The slow clopping of the horse's hoofs continued and, looking over his shoulder, he saw that the growler was still following him. Not only that but the cabby was grinning now as he had when he drove off with Mr. Dennison.

Andrew felt his heart pounding. This couldn't be happening. Someone couldn't be kidnapped in London in daylight—certainly not here in these respectable residential streets. And all at once it occurred to him that that was why the growler had not drawn any closer to him. The cabby was waiting until they got to a different kind of neighborhood, one that was more deserted.

Looking ahead, Andrew saw a nursemaid pushing a pram and he began walking faster. If he kept close to her, he would be safe. Then, when he was still some distance away, she stopped, picked a baby out of the pram and went down into an areaway.

Andrew paused next to the pram, hearing the growler stop behind him. Should he speak to the nanny, tell her what was happening?

Tell her what? As he tried to think of how he could put it, she came out again—a thin woman in a grey uniform and a nurse's cap She looked at him suspiciously, wheeled the pram down into the areaway and went into the house, slamming the iron gate.

The street was deserted now. Behind him Andrew heard the horse's hoofs as the growler started forward, coming towards him, and suddenly he could no longer pretend. He began walking more and more quickly and suddenly he was running—running as fast as he could.

The character of the neighborhood was changing; the houses were smaller, plainer. Then ahead of him he saw traffic. There was the crack of a whip and the horse behind him broke into a trot. He came out on a wide and busy street lined with shops. Without hesitating, he ran in front of an omnibus, under the nose of a horse pulling a dray, and crossed the street. Looking back, he saw the cabby, no longer grinning, trying to work his way through the stream of traffic.

Dodging pedestrians—clerks wearing bowlers, rough-looking men with caps and women carrying shopping baskets—he turned right, then left again. Ahead of him was another street, not quite as wide or busy and, on its far side, a row of wooden sheds. He ran across the street, found a narrow opening between two of the sheds and squeezed through.

He came out into a large open space that faced a

canal where barges were tied up, nose to stern, like a file of sleeping whales. The front of the nearest shed was piled high with bags of coal. He slipped in behind the bags and sat down.

He was panting, and he had a stitch in his side. He tried to breathe more quietly, listening. He could hear the rumble and clatter of traffic behind the shed but nothing else, no sound of footsteps.

He sat there in the quiet darkness of the shed, trying to think. Had Broken Nose seen where he'd gone? At the moment, it didn't seem so. But if he hadn't, how long should he hide there? Certainly for a while.

He moved back until he could lean against the wall. Along with the traffic he heard another sound, oddly discordant, that reminded him of Cornwall. He suddenly realized it was the crying of gulls. Of course. There would be gulls here at the canal basin. Somehow he found that comforting and he began to relax. His eyes closed.

Sitting up with a start, he realized he must have fallen asleep—he did not know for how long. He got up slowly, stiffly, and edged his way past the bags of coal. It had been dark in the shed and now he saw that it was dark outside too, the only light coming from a watchman's shed near the water's edge.

Now what? Should he go back to York Street or to the police? Perhaps now if he told Mrs. Gurney what had happened, she would come to the police station with him. It was worth trying. But first he would have to find his way back to the rooming house.

He squeezed his way between the sheds out to the street. The gaslights were lit now but the street was almost deserted. To his left, he could see a wider street, the one he had crossed before. Traffic was still moving there—he saw a carriage and two hansoms go by—and he started toward it.

He paused when he reached the corner. Farther up the street were some costermongers, selling fruit and vegetables from barrows lit by naptha flares. As he looked at them a voice behind him said, "I thought you might come back this way, Master Andrew."

He whirled. There, standing in the shadow of the building, whip in hand, was the cabby with the broken nose. Andrew stood frozen as he came toward him. Then, as the cabby reached for him, Andrew ducked under his arm and began running again; first toward the costermonger's barrows, then turning sharply, cutting between two of them and across the street. Behind him he heard curses, the shouts of the costermongers as the cabby jostled them.

Running like a frightened hare, Andrew turned right into a dark street, then left into another one. Behind him he heard the pounding of heavy boots. Suddenly he sensed rather than saw a narrow opening; an alley that was even darker than the street. He dodged into it and continued running. At the far end of the alley he could see some dim lights. But before he reached them he ran into something solid but yielding and staggered back.

"Ow! Easy, duck," said a hoarse voice—a woman's voice. "Someone after you?"

"Yes!"

"In here."

Reaching behind her, she opened a door, pulled him in after her and shut the door.

"Quick, Meg," said the woman. "Give me a hand."

A second woman appeared out of the darkness. Andrew could not see her but he could smell the gin on her breath and sensed that she was a big woman, even bigger than the first one.

"It's not the police," he said "It's . . ."

Without warning, he was knocked to the floor. As he lay there, half dazed, he felt fingers unbuttoning his jacket. It was pulled off and so were his trousers, his shirt and tie.

"Get his boots," said the first woman.

"I'm trying to," said the second woman, "but the laces are knotted."

"Well, break them."

His shocked surprise turned into outrage. Drawing back one leg, Andrew lashed out as hard as he could. There was a howl of pain, and he rolled over, got to his knees, his feet, pulled open the door and staggered out into the alley.

He felt as if he were in a nightmare in which he was doomed to run forever up the dark, foul-smelling alley toward the dim glow of distant lights. But he also knew, as he had known for some time, that this was what the world was really like: filled with strangers who would always turn out to be enemies. Then, unsteady on his feet, he tripped, felt himself falling and even the faint lights were gone.

5

Screamer Again

There had been something about a light—he couldn't remember what—his head hurt too much. But when he opened his eyes, there it was. At least, there was *a* light, an oil lamp hanging from a beam in a low ceiling.

As he blinked at it, a voice said, "I think he's coming round, Mum."

He turned his head and found himself lying on a cot. Standing next to it and looking down at him anxiously was Screamer. There were footsteps, and two more faces appeared. He knew one of them: Screamer's brother, Sam. The other was that of a thin woman with greying hair.

"How are you feeling?" she asked.

"I don't know. My head hurts."

"I shouldn't wonder. That was a nasty crack you got."

He raised his hand to his forehead. A rag was tied around it.

"Where am I?"

"Our place," said Screamer.

He looked around. He was in a small room with a table, a stove and a sink.

"But how did I get here?"

"Sam found you, and we brought you up here."

"Found me?"

"You was lying in the courtyard, cold as a kipper and with blood all over your face," said Sam.

"But . . ." He started to sit up, then realized he had

47

nothing on but his drawers and, flushing, pulled up the thin blanket that had been covering him.

Sam nodded grimly. "You'd been stripped," he said. "Did you come through the alley?"

"Yes."

"You shouldn't have. There's some rough judies through there. They're all on the kinchin lay—stealing from young 'uns. But their biggest dodge is rolling drunks and skinning anyone they can handle."

"What were you doing over here anyway?" asked Screamer.

It had all come back to him now; Broken Nose, the women. When he had tripped, fallen, he must have hit his head on the cobbles.

"There was someone after me, chasing me."

"Who?"

"A man. A cabby."

He wished she hadn't asked him that. His head still ached and he was too tired to go through the whole story.

The woman must have sensed that.

"Never mind," she said. "You can tell us in the morning. Go to sleep now."

"He's going to sleep here?" said Sam.

"Yes."

"What happens to me?"

"You can bring in that extra mattress from the bedroom, sleep on that."

Sam scowled at her, at Andrew, then went through a door near the head of the cot. Andrew wanted to protest, say he'd sleep on the mattress, but he couldn't—couldn't even keep his eyes open any longer. He heard a scuffling noise as Sam dragged in the mattress, then nothing more.

A faint clattering woke him. He opened his eyes and saw the grey haired woman busy at the stove. She must, he decided, be Mrs. Wiggins, Screamer's and Sam's mother. She turned, smiled at him. Her face was drawn and careworn, but it was a pleasant smile.

"So you're awake," she said. "How do you feel this morning?"

"Better."

"Good. Do you want to get up? We'll be having breakfast as soon as Sam comes back."

He nodded, started to get up, then remembered that he had no clothes on but his drawers. She saw his hesitation.

"You can wrap yourself in the blanket," she said. "Your boots are under the cot."

She turned her back while he put his shoes on and got up, wrapping himself in the blanket. He had looked around the room quickly the night before. Now he did so again. The room was small and, though it was sparsely furnished, it was clean. The mattress on which Sam had slept—a straw pallet—was on the floor in the corner.

Screamer came in from the bedroom.

"Hello," she said. "Feeling better?"

"Yes."

"Good."

There were footsteps coming up a flight of stairs, the door opened, and Sam came in with a loaf of bread. He looked coldly at Andrew, gave the bread to Mrs. Wiggins. She cut it carefully—two slices for each of them— and poured tea. There were only three rickety chairs at the table, but Screamer brought in a wooden box from the bedroom and Andrew sat on that. The bread was still warm and good, and the tea was strong. There was no milk or sugar on the table, and Andrew did not think he should ask for any. When they had eaten, Mrs. Wiggins said, "All right. Now tell us what happened."

Andrew did, and they listened, Mrs. Wiggins and Screamer with frank—and Sam with grudging— interest.

"Well, I never," said Mrs. Wiggins. "I must say it does sound as if something's not right."

"I dunno," said Sam. "Maybe the man this Mr. Dennison went off with *was* a friend and they sent the cabby to tell him," he jerked his head at Andrew, "where he was."

"Then why didn't he tell him?" asked Screamer.

"He didn't have much of a chance, did he?"

"No," admitted Mrs. Wiggins. "First off, we'd better find out if there's any word from him. And also get Andrew some clothes. Do you have any other clothes?" she asked.

"Yes," said Andrew. "In my bag at Mrs. Gurney's."

"Righto." She turned to Sam. "You run over there, see if there is any word from Mr. Dennison and bring Andrew's bag back here." Then, as he hesitated, "What's wrong? You're not working for Mr. Holmes today, are you?"

"No. But I was going out with my box." And he jerked his head at a shoeshine box near the stove.

"You can go out a little later. Cut along now."

Sam looked at her, at Andrew, then went out reluctantly.

"I've got some marketing to do before I go to work," said Mrs. Wiggins, getting up. "Screamer will keep you company till I get back."

"Yes, ma'am," said Andrew. "Thank you for all the trouble you're taking."

"How could any of us manage if we didn't do what we could for one another?"

Throwing a shawl over her shoulders and picking up a basket, she went out.

"You think that something did happen to Mr. Dennison?" asked Screamer.

"Yes."

"So do I. What do you want to do while we're waiting?"

"I don't know. What can we do?"

"Will you read to me?"

"If you like. Do you have something to read?"

"I don't, but Sam does."

She reached under the cot, brought out a crumpled penny dreadful and gave it to him. He had read many of them himself, much to his Aunt Agnes' annoyance, but this was one he had not seen before. It was titled *The Boy Detective*, and the lurid cover showed a boy crouching behind a barrel and watching a cloaked figure that stood at the end of a dock in silhouette against a full moon. Again Andrew felt a twinge of jealousy. Though he had read about detectives, Sam not only knew one but actually worked with him.

Opening the book, he said, "I'll read it to you if you read the first page to me."

Screamer squirmed uncomfortably. "I can't."

"Of course you can. You did very well at the zoo. Try it. I'll help you."

"All right." In an uncertain voice, she began, " 'The thick yellow fog crept in from the river. Tom walked up the middle of the dark street listening to the lapping of the water in the . . .' " She hesitated.

"Distance."

"Distance." She went on, pausing occasionally but gaining confidence, until she reached the bottom of the page.

"That was very good," said Andrew.

"Was it? All right. Now you."

She gave him the book, pressed close to him, eyes on the well-thumbed pages, as he continued the story. He had almost finished it when there were footsteps on the stairs. Snatching the book from him, Screamer hid it under the cot again. The door opened, and Sam and Mrs. Wiggins came in together.

"Where's the bag?" asked Screamer.

"Tell them," said Mrs. Wiggins.

"The landlady almost called the coppers when I told her I was there for you," said Sam to Andrew. "She said a man stopped by last night with a note from Mr. Dennison saying as how he was sick and staying with a friend—the man who brought the note—and so were you."

"The note said I was with him?" said Andrew.

"Yes."

"What kind of a man was this?"

"A young 'un. Why?"

"I wondered if it was the cabby."

"No. The landlady said he was a gentleman, real well spoken. Anyway the note asked if she'd please give the man Mr. Dennison's bag and yours, and it said just what they looked like, so she did."

"Well, there you are," said Andrew. "That proves something's wrong."

"How?"

"Well, I'm not with Mr. Dennison. That means the whole thing is a lie."

"Maybe not the whole thing," said Sam. "Maybe your Mr. Dennison *is* sick and is staying with a friend."

"Then why did he say I was with him."

"I dunno."

"I think Andrew's right," said Mrs. Wiggins. "I think something is wrong and he'd better talk to the police. The thing is, what's he going to do until they find his Mr. Dennison?"

"He'll stay here with us," said Screamer.

"You're balmy!" said Sam. "He can't do that."

"Why not?"

"Because we don't have the room."

"He can sleep on the mattress there."

"And what about food? You know we just about get along as it is."

"Mum!" said Screamer, looking at her mother pleadingly.

"I'm sorry, but Sam's right," said Mrs. Wiggins unhappily. "I feel bad about it because I like Andrew too—he's a nice boy—but I don't know how we could manage. I'm sure if he goes to the police, they'll take care of him, find some place for him to stay."

"No!" said Screamer.

"Now, Sara," Mrs. Wiggins began.

Screamer screamed. She closed her eyes, her body went stiff, and she screamed so loudly and piercingly that the sound was like a physical blow. Mrs. Wiggins and Sam both flinched.

"Screamer, stop that!" said Mrs. Wiggins sharply.

She stopped only long enough to take a deep breath, then screamed again, even louder.

"You heard Mum!" shouted Sam. "Stop that or I'll belt you!" and he raised a threatening hand.

Screamer ignored him, and Andrew backed away. It seemed impossible for that sound to come from such a small, thin body—impossible for it to continue at that volume and pitch—but it did. Mrs. Wiggins and Sam both had their hands to their ears now. Mrs. Wiggins looked helplessly at Sam.

"All right! All right!" she said finally. "You're giving me a headache and busting my eardrums. He can stay."

"Mum!" said Sam.

"Don't you start giving me trouble, too. I said he can stay. For a while anyway."

"Sure," said Sam bitterly. "We'll all just eat less. And what about clothes? *I* ain't got nothing I can give him."

"I'll get him some clothes," said Screamer.

"Where?"

"Where you get yours when you need 'em. From the Samaritan Society or the Salvation Army."

"All right. He's your friend. You take care of him. I'm off." And picking up his shoeshine box he went out, slamming the door behind him.

"You mustn't mind Sam," said Mrs. Wiggins to Andrew. "He's not mean or anything like that. It's just that things have been hard since Mr. Wiggins died. And even worse lately because I haven't been too well myself, haven't been able to do as much work as I used to. But one way or another, we'll manage."

"No," said Andrew. "If Screamer can get me some clothes, I'll go."

"Go where? You don't have anyone else; know anyone else in London, do you?"

"No."

"Then you'll stay here with us till we get this sorted out. Now I've got to go myself. The lady I char for has company coming for lunch and wanted me in early. I'll

53

see you both tonight." And wrapping herself in her shawl, she left.

"You're not angry, are you?" asked Screamer anxiously.

"At what?"

"At the way Sam acted. Like Mum said, he worries."

"No, I'm not angry."

"That's good. He'll come around. I'll go get some clothes for you. If they've got any at the Samaritan Society, I shouldn't be long. You'll be all right, won't you?"

"Yes. I'll be all right."

When the door closed, he went to the window and looked out. There was a cobbled courtyard below. To the right was the narrow alley through which he had come the night before. To the left was a wider passage that must lead out to the street. As he watched, Screamer came out into the courtyard, waved to someone and hurried out through the passage.

He remained there after she had disappeared, trying to decide how he felt. Certainly no worse than he had the day before. He had been completely alone then, with no one to talk to—no one who cared the least bit about him. Not only that but he had been threatened in a way and for reasons he could not comprehend. Now, for the moment at least, he was safe. More important, he had a friend—and perhaps more than one. For he believed that Mrs. Wiggins did like him as she had said she did. As for Sam, he was probably a little jealous for several reasons, particularly because of the way Screamer felt about him. But in time he might get over it as Mrs. Wiggins had said he would. So much for the present. As for the future, that was still dark, obscure. He had no idea what was going to become of him. But despite that, it seemed that there *had* been a dim light at the end of the alley after all.

As he stood there, he heard a strangely familiar sound—a horse stamping his hoofs—and he realized he had heard it several times before without recognizing it. But once he did, he became aware of the not too unpleasant smell of manure that went with it. There must be a stable nearby.

When Screamer came back she was carrying a bundle of clothes.

"I hope these'll do," she said, handing them over. "They didn't have too much there."

He looked at them. There was a jacket and trousers that didn't match and were quite worn and not too clean. There was a shirt that was clean—it had been washed—but had no collar.

"Thanks," he said. "I'll go inside and put them on."

"Why inside?" she asked. And when he didn't answer, "You are a nellie. I got a brother, haven't I? But go ahead."

He went into the other room, which had a bed and a chest of drawers in it. He dropped the blanket that he had wrapped around him and put on the clothes. The shirt fit well enough, but the jacket and trousers were both too big. He folded up the trouser bottoms so they would not drag on the ground and went back into the kitchen, holding them up.

"I don't suppose you have a belt, do you?" he asked.

"No. But I think we've got some string."

She found some heavy twine in the drawer of the kitchen table and gave it to him. When he had tied it around his waist, securing his trousers, Screamer studied him.

"Well, they're not exactly like your own things," she said, "but they're clothes. And you've got your boots. They're the hardest things to get. Now what?"

"I suppose I'd better go to the police."

"You suppose?" She looked at him shrewdly. "You don't like this Mr. Dennison much, do you?"

"No," he admitted.

"Then why are you going to do it?"

"Well, I can't just let him disappear and not do anything about it," he said. There was something else of course. Mr. Dennison was the one link he had to his past, someone who had talked to Aunt Agnes, and, though he had never said anything about it, might know something about his mother.

"All right," said Screamer. "I'll go with you."

They went out and down a flight of rickety stairs. Under the Wiggins's rooms and taking up most of that side of the courtyard was a stable. A sign over the open door said DINGELL'S LIVERY, and sitting on a nail keg in front of it and mending a harness was a stout, red-faced man. He nodded to Screamer as they went by. Andrew hesitated, then on an impulse went over to him.

"Excuse me, sir," he said. "Could you use a boy to help out here?"

"What makes you think I need a boy?"

"I just thought I'd ask."

The man looked him up and down.

"Do you know horses?"

"Yes, sir."

"How?"

"I used to help out in a blacksmith's shop in Cornwall."

In a sense, it was true. When he had stopped by at Trefethen's, he had not only worked the bellows at the forge but had helped out with the horses, too. And he did like them.

The man grunted skeptically. Putting down the harness, he jerked his head at Andrew and led the way into the stable. There was a bony, black horse in one of the stalls.

"Bring that one out," he said.

"Wait a minute," said Screamer. "Isn't he the mean one?"

"So? He's got to be handled, ain't he?" Then to Andrew, "Well?"

"Yes, sir."

He stepped into the stall, and the horse stamped his hoofs and turned his head, the white of his eyes showing.

"Easy, boy," said Andrew soothingly, putting his hand on the horse's flank. He whistled softly through his teeth in the way he had learned from Trefethen and worked his way in between the horse and the side of the stall. There was a raw place on the horse's shoulder, and he was careful not to touch it. He stroked the horse's head sympathetically, untied the halter and backed him out.

"He's got a bad harness gall," he said, pointing to the sore.

"Why do you think he's here instead of out pulling a cab?" said the man. "What's your name?"

Andrew hesitated. He didn't know if the cabby with the broken nose was still looking for him. Somehow he doubted it. But even if he was, it was unlikely that he'd recognize him in the clothes he was wearing. On the other hand, he had known his name. And if he should come around this neighborhood asking for him . . .

With her usual quickness Screamer guessed what was troubling him and did something about it.

"His name's Jack," she said. "He's my cousin."

"I'm Lem Dingell. As it happens, my regular boy is sick, and I can use someone to help out until he gets back. It's hard work. Besides helping with the horses, you'll do all the mucking out. But I'll pay ninepence a day."

"Ninepence?" said Screamer. "You pay Harry a bob!"

"How do you know that?"

"Because he told me."

Dingell glowered at her, then turned back to Andrew.

"All right. I'll give you a bob, too. Be here at six tomorrow morning."

"Yes, sir."

"A bob a day," said Screamer as they started across the courtyard. "That's as much as Sam makes, except when he's working for Mr. Holmes. What are you going to do with it?"

"What do you think? I wasn't sure I'd find anything—at least not this fast—but I wasn't going to stay with you if I couldn't help out."

"You mean you're going to give it to Mum?"

57

"Of course."

"That's what I thought, but I wanted to make sure." A rapt expression came over her face. "Lumme! You know what that means? With an extra bob a day we can have meat twice a week."

6

Meeting on King Street

"I didn't realize that you were interested in Oriental art," said Watson.

"Homo sum," said Holmes. *"Humani nil a me alienum puto."*

"That's quite true. Nothing does seem alien to you. Still, Oriental art . . ."

"As usual, you give me too much credit. I neither know nor am I interested in all forms of Oriental art. But I am interested in netsuke."

"Chinese carvings, aren't they?"

"Japanese. Very human as well as imaginative. Used to hang things from a man's sash. I'll tell you more about them when we get inside."

They had turned into King Street from St. James and he had almost reached Christie and Manson's Auction Rooms when a tall, fair man in a tweed suit came out.

"Lytell!" called Holmes. Then, as the man turned and came toward them with a smile, "Though I suppose I should now say 'My Lord' or 'Your Lordship'."

"You should not. I'm still not used to it, and I don't like it. Please keep it Lytell."

"As you wish."

"It's nice to see you again, Holmes. You too, Dr. Watson. You've both been very much on my mind, and I've been rather expecting to hear from you."

"About what?" asked Holmes.

"Well, it's been almost a fortnight since I came to see you. I thought one or both of you would send me a bill."

"We did nothing to warrant sending you a bill."

"I disagree. You did a great deal. You went to see Dr. Harvey Moore, ascertained the facts concerning my father's death and reassured me about it."

"We were happy to do it," said Watson. "Have you had any more attacks since then?"

"No, doctor. I haven't. So I saw no need to consult a specialist in nervous disorders as you suggested."

"Very sensible," said Holmes. "One of the best ways to stay well is to avoid doctors. We saw you come out of Christie and Manson's. Were you at the viewing?"

"You mean for the auction tomorrow? No, I had other business there. I've just completed arrangements with them to sell some paintings."

"Family paintings?"

"In a sense. One of them is the Reynolds portrait of Lady Lydia. The others are ones my father bought many years ago. A Carvaggio, a Rubens and a Constable. The old boy did have rather good taste. Or good advice."

"It certainly sounds like it. But why are you doing it?"

"Because I have to. While the estate is quite large, there doesn't seem to be very much ready cash, and I need quite a bit for the death duties and for repairs."

"At Lowther Hall?"

"No, no. I don't care about that. I'll probably close the place up. But the tenants' cottages are in shocking shape—leaking roofs, cracked and crumbling walls—I'm afraid my father was a rather typical landlord in that respect, and I want to have them all fixed up."

"Very estimable of you."

"Not at all. My father seemed to feel very little responsibility towards the tenants, but I feel a great deal."

"Still, to sell paintings that have been in the family for some time . . ."

"I know. I don't like the idea, but it seemed preferable to selling off any of the land. I sent a cable to my younger brother in the United States asking him how he felt about it, and I just received an answer telling me to go ahead, so I did."

"I see."

"Look, since neither of you has sent me a bill and apparently don't intend to, can I take you both out to dinner and perhaps the theatre afterward?"

"It's very kind of you, but I'm afraid we can't make it tonight. We're going to Sarasate's concert at St. James Hall."

"Oh. Well, I'm going down to Norby Cross tomorrow with a photographer. Christie and Manson want photographs of the paintings for their catalogue. But could we make it when I get back?"

"I don't see why not."

"Splendid! I'll be back on Friday, get in touch with you then." And shaking hands with both of them, he went off up King Street.

"Well, I must say that a title doesn't seem to have changed him any," said Watson.

"I didn't expect it would," said Holmes. "He's a thoroughly decent chap."

"Yes, he is. Still I wish he had consulted someone about that attack of his. Even though he hasn't had another one, I don't like the fact that it was never diagnosed or explained."

"But the explanation for it is obvious," said Holmes in his most offhand way. "He was drugged."

Watson stared at him.

"Drugged? With what? Neither cannabis nor opium would have made him act the way he did."

"They're not the only drugs in the pharmacopoeia. What about peyote?"

"I've never heard of it."

"Your interests do not run as far afield as mine. It's made from the button of a particular kind of cactus and is much used by Mexican and American Indian medicine men. It causes hallucinations, loss of the time sense and sometimes acute anxiety—all the symptoms that Lytell described when he came to see us."

Watson shook his head.

"Holmes, you never cease to amaze me!"

"Because I happen to be familiar with a drug that you don't know?"

"For many reasons. But who could have given him that drug? And why?"

"I can always count on you to ask the pertinent questions," said Holmes with a smile. "However, I'm afraid I can't answer them. Not yet."

"But you have some ideas?"

"I always have ideas. But I don't base my conclusions on them or on speculations, but on facts. And since we don't have enough of them at the moment to warrant anything but a theory, we shall have to be patient."

7

Two More Cases for Holmes

"If there are any more, I think I probably will be," said Holmes, rubbing some rosin on his bow.

"It would certainly make sense," said Watson. "I can't think of anyone . . ." He dropped the newspaper and stared at Holmes. "You probably will be what?"

"Approached by the authorities on last night's bombing."

"How on earth did you know that's what I was thinking about?"

Holmes smiled.

"You know my methods, Watson."

"Yes, I do, but . . . Are you saying you read my mind again—followed my thoughts—merely by observing me?"

"It would appear so, would it not?"

"But how?"

"You were properly shocked when we heard about it last night, commented on the fact that it was so close to us, and wondered about the details. My assumption was that that was the first thing you read when you picked up the paper."

"That's correct."

"You then glanced at your bag, and it seemed fairly clear to me that you were thinking that if we had been home instead of out with Lytell, and if the bomb had gone off earlier and many people had been hurt, you might have been called on to help. And you wondered whether you had everything you needed in your bag to do so."

"Correct also."

"You then went back to the paper, which I suspect talked about 'eighty-one, the year we met and the year when the Dynamiters were most active. You then paused and glanced at your desk. That is where you write the somewhat colorful accounts of my cases—and it seemed logical to assume that you were trying to remember whether I had been called in to help solve those earlier bombings. As it happens, I wasn't. I was not particularly well known then. But now of course I am—so when you turned and looked at me, it seemed reasonable to suppose that you were wondering whether this time I would be called in."

"Well, now that you've explained it, I must say that it does seem rather obvious."

"Of course," said Holmes dryly. "In fact, elementary." And raising his violin he began playing the opening of the Kreutzer Sonata that they had heard Sarasate play three nights before.

There was a knock, and their landlady opened the door.

"Yes, Mrs. Hudson?"

"A young lady to see you, sir," she said. "She has no appointment, but . . ."

"It doesn't matter," said Holmes, putting down his violin. "Show her in."

Mrs. Hudson stepped aside, and a soberly dressed, attractive, dark-haired woman in her early thirties entered. Her face was anxious, troubled, and she looked uncertainly from Holmes to Watson.

"Mr. Holmes?"

"I am Holmes. This is my good friend, Dr. Watson."

"I'm Margaret Harker. It's good of you to see me this way. I know I should have made an appointment, but I only arrived in London last night . . ."

"From the United States?"

"Yes. I suppose it's obvious that I'm an American."

"And also that you're extremely distressed. Please sit down and tell me how I can help you."

"You're very kind," she said, sitting gracefully in the chair he held for her. "You can indeed help me if you will agree to."

"And why should I not?"

"Because . . ." She looked at Watson.

"Dr. Watson is not only my friend but has been involved in many of my cases. You can speak freely in front of him."

"Very well. Though I do not believe this is the kind of case you are generally consulted about."

"I have been consulted about some very strange ones." He glanced at the ring on her left hand. "It's Mrs. Harker, is it not?"

"Yes, I'm married. That is an important part of my problem."

"Perhaps you had better begin at the beginning and give me all the details."

"I will give you the essential ones and then, if you wish, you can ask me questions. Have you ever heard of John Harker?"

"I'm afraid not. Your husband?"

"Yes. I thought his name might be familiar to you since he is quite well known in American financial circles. I don't know much about his early history except that he comes from Chicago, where he was involved in railroads. When he came to New York, he was already quite wealthy."

"You are from New York yourself?"

"Yes. My maiden name was de Windt. We're quite an old family—I think that's one of the things that interested John—but we were by no means rich. Though he is considerably older than I am, when I first met him I was rather attracted to him. He's a very striking looking, masterful man, and after several months of quite intense courtship, I married him."

"How long ago was this?"

"Ten years ago. Within a few weeks I realized it was a mistake. He did not love me, was not interested in anything but his financial dealings, and wanted—not so much a wife—as a well-bred and accomplished hostess for his very lavish dinners and parties. Well, I did what was expected of me dutifully and, I think, well, and after we had been married for a year I had a child—a girl we named Rachel after my mother—and that changed things completely."

"In what way?"

"My life finally had some meaning. John cared no more about Rachel than he did about me—I think if we had had a boy it might have been different—but she was everything to me. Everything!" Her deep, warm voice became even deeper with emotion. "Though we had a nurse, I spent almost all my time with Rachel. She was a wonderful baby, an even more wonderful child—sensitive, intelligent and loving and . . . I don't think I need to tell you about her."

"No," said Holmes.

"During the years that followed, my husband was away a good deal and I began to hear stories about him and other women." She smiled a little wryly. "One can always count on one's friends for that. I paid no attention to the stories. I had Rachel, and I had never really had John, so what did it matter? Then, about two months ago, Rachel and I came home unexpectedly from a visit with friends in Newport and found John in our home with his latest flame, a dancer. She had apparently been there all the time we were away. This was too much. I did not mind his affairs when they were discreet. But to flaunt his mistress in our own house, in front of the servants . . . I asked him to leave, and the next day I consulted an attorney about a divorce."

"There was no question about evidence, I gather," said Holmes.

"None. The servants were all willing to testify on my behalf. Then, about a week later . . ." her voice broke, "Rachel disappeared."

"Disappeared?" said Watson.

She nodded, her face strained. "John had picked her up at school, saying I was ill. That night I got a note from him in which he said that since I had kept him from Rachel for all these years—which was not true— he was going to keep her from me. That I would never see her again."

"But this is monstrous!" said Watson indignantly. "Didn't you go to the police?"

"Of course. They investigated, discovered that John had sailed for France that afternoon with Rachel and then told me something that you are probably aware of, Mr. Holmes, but which staggered me. They said that John had done nothing illegal. That since he was Rachel's father, it was not kidnapping, and there was nothing I could do about it."

"That's correct," said Holmes. "But I gather you did not leave matters at that."

"No, I did not. I engaged private detectives. They determined that John is now at the Claridge in Paris with Rachel and that he has employed two bodyguards to watch her. When I heard that, I immediately came here to London to see you."

"Why me?" asked Holmes.

"Surely that is obvious. You are said to be—and I believe you are—the cleverest detective in the world. I am not a rich woman, Mr. Holmes, but I have some means—and I will strip myself of everything I have to get my child back!"

"In other words," said Holmes slowly, "you would like me to do what your husband did—steal your child and return her to you."

"Exactly. He does not love her. He never loved her. He took her for only one reason—to hurt me. But if it was not illegal for him to do what he did, it cannot be illegal for me to do it either."

"There is a difference. He is the child's father. I am not. And even though I did it on your behalf, the case is not the same."

"I'm aware of that. And also of the difficulties. Apart from the bodyguards, John will probably move, go somewhere else and take another name. But if there is anyone who can find him, get Rachel away from him and restore her to me, it is you. Will you do it? Will you?"

She clasped her hands, looking at Holmes imploringly.

"It's an interesting case," he said. "I don't recall another exactly like it." He thought a moment. "You say you arrived in London last night?"

"Yes."

"Where are you staying?"

"At a boarding house in St. John's Wood—Twelve Henry Street. It was recommended to me by a friend in New York."

"But you've been to London before."

"No, never."

"Are you sure?"

"Of course I'm sure!"

"There's no need to get shirty about it," he said pacifically.

"But I'm not getting . . . I beg your pardon?"

"I'm sorry. I meant upset. As I said, it's an interesting case. Unfortunately, however, I am presently involved in two others that are quite important. I shall have to let you know whether I can undertake this one for you."

"But you must!" she said desperately, pathetically. "I'm sure Rachel is almost as frightened and miserable as I am. Is there nothing I can do to persuade you to help me?"

"I'm afraid not, Mrs. Harker. I'm aware of your deep feelings in the matter, but I must see what I can do about my other commitments. I will let you know my answer as soon as I can."

"Then I suppose I must wait," she said. "Wait and pray." She rose, trying to conceal her distress and disappointment. "Thank you for your patience, Mr. Holmes."

"Not at all."

He opened the door for her and, bowing to him and Watson, she left.

"Well, Watson?" said Holmes, returning to the couch and picking up his violin again.

"A very moving and truly tragic story. I did not realize that you were involved in two other cases."

"I'm not."

"But you said . . ."

"I said so because I wanted some time to think about it."

"But what is there to think about? I'm aware that what she wants you to do would be very difficult . . ."

"You think that is why I did not agree to take the case?"

"I can't think of any other reason."

"In other words, you believe that I should help her."

"Yes, I do. I would certainly do so if she had asked me for help. I have never seen a woman as deeply and sincerely moved as she was when she talked about her child."

"Nor have I. She did seem quite affected. And I found that very interesting—almost as interesting as the flaws in her story."

"Flaws?"

"She claimed to be an American. She has certainly lived in America, but I will wager anything you like that she was born in London—probably in Lambeth."

"What? That's ridiculous, Holmes! How can you say that?"

"Because I have an ear, Watson—a very good and well trained ear—and I detected the remnants of Cockney vowels in her cultivated and quite excellent speech."

"Well, I may not have your musical ear, but I have known Americans too, and I heard nothing of the sort!"

"There's little point in debating it. I have studied speech as I have studied many other things and I can locate anyone's origin in England within a few miles. Besides, if she is not a Londoner, has never been here before, how do you account for her reaction to the word 'shirty'?"

"As I recall it—and I recall it clearly because I was surprised to hear you use such common slang—she did not know what you meant."

"So she said—*after* she had reacted to it. But you have made your position quite clear. You were impressed by her, believe her implicitly and feel that I should help her."

"Yes, I do."

"Well, you've always been rather susceptible to female charm," said Holmes and, picking up his violin again, he began playing an intricate pizzicato cadenza. As Watson stared, trying to decide exactly what Holmes meant by that, there was another, perfunctory knock, the door opened and a large, leonine man came in.

"Ah, Gregory," said Holmes. "We've been expecting you."

Gregory paused in midstride.

"But that's impossible. I just left the Yard, did not expect to come here myself until a few minutes ago."

"Doing easily what others find difficult is talent. Doing what is impossible is genius."

"I see," said Gregory, smiling. "You're joking with me. Well, I don't mind. I just saw a rather attractive lady leaving. One of your clients?"

"That's something Watson and I were just discussing. You know Watson, of course?"

"Of course. Good morning, doctor."

"Inspector . . ." said Watson bowing.

"Now tell us what brings you here with such mixed feelings," said Holmes.

"How do you know that is how I feel?"

Holmes smiled. "It's fortunate that the career you chose was enforcing the law rather than the opposite. Your face is as easy to read as a newspaper."

"Is it? Then perhaps you can tell me why my feelings are mixed."

"I think I can. I've helped Scotland Yard, and you personally, on several cases. I know that you think very highly of my abilities. So I suspect that if you resent having had to come and ask for my help today—as I think you have—it is because you think you can handle the matter yourself. But since you *did* come, I would guess that someone else, someone with considerable authority, insisted that you do so."

Gregory's blue eyes widened.

"You know, Mr. Holmes, you could make a fortune on the stage reading minds. Would you like to go a step further and tell me what I've come to see you about?"

"I suspect it's yesterday's bombing in the Baker Street Underground station."

Gregory continued to stare at him for a moment, then slapped his thigh.

"Mr. Holmes, no matter how high my regard for you is, it's clear I don't regard you highly enough."

"That goes without saying," said Holmes with only the slightest touch of irony. "Then I'm right? It is about the bombing?"

"It is. What do you know about it?"

"Just that there was an explosion at about eight o'clock last night and the ticket taker was injured—not seriously, I gather."

"That's correct."

"Was anyone else hurt?" asked Watson.

"No, doctor. Luckily the bombing took place at an off hour."

"I suppose there's no question but that it was a bomb and not a gas explosion or anything of that sort," said Holmes.

"None," said Gregory. "We found the remnants of the clockwork that set it off. But that's not all. Shortly before that we found two other bombs—packages of dynamite with timing mechanisms—one at the British Museum and the other at the Tate Gallery."

"What?" said Watson. "There was nothing about that in the paper."

"No. It was impossible to do anything about the explosion in the Underground. But since we found the others before they could go off, we were able to hush up any mention of them. Nevertheless, as you can see, the matter does look serious."

"What you're afraid of," said Holmes, "is that the Dynamiters may be at it again."

"Exactly. And that is why I was instructed to come and see you and give you this." And he took an envelope from his pocket and gave it to Holmes.

He glanced at it and raised an eyebrow.

"From Ten Downing Street," he said. He opened the envelope, read the note that was in it, then handed it to Watson who read it also.

"This is quite extraordinary, Holmes," said Watson. "I know you have had communications from the Home Secretary, but have you ever been appealed to before by the Prime Minister himself?"

"No," said Holmes.

"Of course you'll do it," said Gregory. "You will help us find out who is responsible for these bombings so that they can be stopped before they get completely out of hand."

"I don't know," said Holmes. "I shall have to think about it."

"You're not serious!" said Gregory. "What's there to think about?"

"Several things. As it happens, I'm engaged in another case. I'll have to let you know if I can become involved in this one also."

"But what can possibly be as important as this one?" asked Gregory. "You know what happened in the early eighties. We had so many men trying to combat the Dynamiters that it became a holiday for other criminals."

"I remember it well," said Holmes.

"And there's nothing I can do to persuade you?"

"I'm afraid not. As I said, I will let you know if I can take on the case."

"I see," said Gregory. "I will tell that to the Commissioner and let him communicate it to the Prime Minister." And nodding rather coldly to Holmes, he left.

"I must say I find this hard to understand, Holmes," said Watson. "Was the other case you were referring to that of Mrs. Harker?"

"Yes."

"But how can you possibly compare them? This one is important enough for the Prime Minister himself to ask you to look into it, while the other is of no importance at all!"

"Except to Mrs. Harker. And just a few minutes ago you were urging me to help her."

"But that was before you were asked to help put a stop to the bombings. I confess that your reasoning baffles me."

"Not for the first time, Watson. And probably not for the last. I will point out to you that even if I do not become involved in the matter of the bombings, they will not be ignored. All of Scotland Yard will be mobilized to find out who was responsible for them. But if I do not help Mrs. Harker, no one else will."

"But I thought you had some serious doubts about her story."

"I do have. And that is one of the reasons I am inclined to take on her case." He rose. "I'm going out. Would you care to come with me?"

"If you'd like me to," said Watson, a bit stiffly.

"You know I always enjoy your company," said Holmes with a smile.

Only partly mollified, Watson got his hat and stick and they went out. Holmes looked right and left—at the passersby, the window shoppers, and the grey-haired beggar who stood near the corner—then crossed the street and entered Jonathan Walker's shop.

Walker was in his office, but when he saw Holmes he came out.

"I'm delighted to see you again, Mr. Holmes," he said. "And you, Dr. Watson."

"We were passing by, and I thought I'd stop in and find out if you have had any more difficulties since your fire."

"No, I have not. I went to see Inspector Gregory as you suggested. He said that several other, similar cases had been reported and that he would look into it. Since then I have not been troubled."

"Whoever is responsible undoubtedly knows that you

went to the police, and your resolute stand must have made him think twice about harassing you further. It would be interesting to know who was behind the conspiracy—and the police may find out eventually—but in the meantime I doubt if you will be troubled again."

"I agree with you. And I thank you for your advice."

"It was nothing. There is, however, something you can do for me. Do you remember my asking you about the Second Bruch Concerto?"

"I do indeed. I told you I knew a dealer in Paris who might have it and said that I would inquire the next time I went there. Unfortunately I have not been there since."

"I suspected that. But, as it happens, I'm going there myself tomorrow on a case, and I wondered if you could give me his name so that I could ask him about it."

"I'll be delighted to," said Walker. And taking a notebook from his pocket, he wrote something in it, tore out the page, and gave it to Holmes.

"Hassler, Twelve Rue de Rivoli," said Holmes, reading it. "I thank you."

"Not at all. Will you be gone for long?"

"It's hard to say. It will be for at least a week, perhaps longer."

"Well, I wish you success, both on your case and on your search for the concerto."

"I thank you for that too," said Holmes. "I'll undoubtedly see you when I return."

"I shall look forward to it," said Walker.

"Well," said Watson when they were outside, "it appears that you have made up your mind and are going to take Mrs. Harker's case."

"Yes, I am. I'll leave for Paris the first thing in the morning."

"I still don't understand why, but I suppose you must do as you think best."

"I usually do."

"Yes, I know. I gather you do not wish me to come with you."

"I think, in this case, I will do better alone. I have several things to do now. I must make my travel arrangements, see Mrs. Harker, and get descriptions of her husband and daughter. But after that I will be free. Shall we meet and have dinner at the Café Royal?"

"You know I do not care particularly for French food," said Watson. "But I suppose you have a reason for that too, such as practising your French. Very well. I'll meet you there at eight."

8

Blind Ben

Screamer was peeling potatoes at the kitchen table when Andrew came in. She looked up and smiled, then looked at him again and said, "What's up?"

"I'm through at Dingell's."

"You got the sack?"

He nodded.

"Why?"

"His old boy, Harry, is coming back and he won't be needing me."

"Well, he said it would just be for a while—until Harry did come back."

"I know."

"Don't let your chin hang down. You'll get something else."

"And if I don't?"

"We'll manage."

He shook his head. He knew now how important every penny was in the Wiggins household.

"I won't stay if I'm not bringing anything in."

"What'll you do?"

"I don't know. Probably go back to Cornwall."

Her small, white face became even paler.

"But you can't do that. You've got no one there—no family or friends."

"There's Jack Trefethen."

"You said you didn't know if he'd let you stay with him. Besides, what about Mr. Dennison?"

"There's been no word from the police. That means they haven't found him."

"The sergeant said it'd take time, and it's only been a little over a week. But let's not talk about it now. Let's see what Mum and Sam have to say about it."

"All right. Can I help with the potatoes?"

"No. Tell me about Cornwall."

He should have expected it. Whenever they were alone—whenever he wasn't reading to her or making her read—she wanted him to tell her about Cornwall.

"Why do you like hearing about it so much?"

"I dunno. I just do."

"What would you like me to tell you about it?"

"I don't care. The sea."

For some reason, perhaps because she had never seen it, that was what she liked best. And so he told her about it again: how clear and clean and blue it was in the early morning; how the pebbles on the shingle beach gleamed when the tide was ebbing and what the fishing boats looked like as they went out. He was telling her about the birds—the gulls and terns and the shags that roosted on the rocks offshore—when Mrs. Wiggins came home. She looked grave when they told her what had happened.

"Ah, well," she said. "We knew it was only temporary. And it wasn't 'cause you didn't give satisfaction. Mr. Dingell said you was very good with the horses."

"He was," said Screamer. "He was better than Harry. But what'll we do now? Andrew says he won't stay if he's not bringing anything in."

"Well, I'm not saying the extra money wasn't a help. It was. Maybe Sam's heard of something else for you, Andrew. He sometimes does."

Sam was late that night. They could tell from the way he dropped his shoebox when he came in that he hadn't had a good day, but still he didn't seem as concerned as they had expected when they told him the news.

"As it happens, there is something," he said slowly. "I heard about it this morning. It's not easy work and I don't know how long it'll last, but the money's good, better than Dingell was paying."

"Doing what, Sam?" asked Mrs. Wiggins.

"Leading a blind man."

"If the pay's so good," said Screamer, "why don't you do it yourself?"

"Because I'm going to be busy doing something else—something for Mr. Holmes."

"Working with him?" asked Andrew.

"Even the Irregulars don't work *with* Mr. Holmes. We work *for* him. Besides, he's not even here now. He left for Paris this morning. But that's got nothing to do with you. Now do you want the job or don't you?"

"Of course I want it," said Andrew. "When do I start?"

"Tomorrow morning. You won't be able to live here with us. You'll have to stay with this blind man, Ben—look after him, cook for him and all that."

"Oh," said Screamer, disappointed. "Well, it'll only be for a while, won't it?"

"Yes," said Sam.

"Where will I find him?" asked Andrew.

"I'll take you to him," said Sam. "But there's another thing." He studied Andrew. "Your clothes is all right, but your hair's not. We'll have to cut it."

"Oh, no!" said Screamer. "Why?"

"Because he looks too much like a toff. Go borrow Mrs. Wagner's scissors, Screamer."

"I won't!" said Screamer. "He has beautiful hair!"

"It gets cut, or he don't get the job," said Sam flatly.

"Please get the scissors, Screamer," said Andrew.

Screamer went out reluctantly and came back a few minutes later with a pair of shears. She closed her eyes while Sam cut Andrew's hair. The Wigginses had no mirror, so Andrew couldn't see how he looked but, when he ran his hand over his head afterwards, he could tell that it had been cropped as closely as Sam's.

Breakfast the next morning was a quiet meal. Screamer kept glancing at Andrew and looking as if she might cry, and Mrs. Wiggins was solemn when she said goodbye and told him to take care of himself. Then Andrew and Sam left.

They went out through the passage, over to Edgeware Road and along it toward Hyde Park. Sam, carrying his shoeshine box, was silent, and Andrew said nothing to him until they had almost reached the Marble Arch when he asked, "Where are we meeting him?"

Sam jerked his chin. A man stood on the corner across from the Arch with his back to them. He wore a long, dark cloak, a wide-brimmed, black felt hat and his grey hair hung down almost to his shoulders. He must have been tall when he was younger, but now he was stooped and leaned on a blackthorn stick. As they approached him, he turned . . . and Andrew shuddered. He had seen blind men before, but never one like this. His eyes were not merely sightless; they were milky white, red-rimmed and ravaged. But, in spite of his blank stare, there was something fierce and proud about him that seemed to reject and defy sympathy.

"Wiggins?" he said.

"Yes, sir," said Sam.

"My name's Ben, Blind Ben," said the man, speaking with a decided Irish brogue. "Is the boy with you?"

"Right here."

"Come closer, boy," said Ben.

Andrew stepped forward and saw that the blind man had a battered fiddle under his left arm. He transferred his stick to his left hand, reached out and ran the fingers of his right hand over Andrew's face. They were strong, sensitive fingers, and Andrew did not know what they told him.

Finally the man grunted. "Are you willing to come with me and stay with me for a while?" he asked.

"Yes, sir," said Andrew.

"I said my name's Ben! What's yours?"

"Andrew. Andrew Craigie."

"And where are you from?"

"Gorlyn in Cornwall."

Ben grunted again. "All right," he said. "You'll do. We'll go now." And without another word to Sam, he turned and started along Oxford Street, tapping the pavement ahead of him with his stick.

When they reached Orchard Street, a green "Atlas"

80

bus came toward them from Baker Street. Still tapping, Ben stepped off the curb.

"Wait, sir," said Andrew and, taking him by the arm, he pulled him back.

"Will you stop calling me 'sir'?" said Ben angrily. "I told you my name's Ben. What is it?"

"There was a bus coming."

"Oh. Yes. I keep forgetting." He stood there for a moment. "Is this Orchard Street?"

"Yes."

"Hold these," he said, handing Andrew his stick and his hat. Then, tucking the fiddle under his chin, he began to play. He played extremely well but, after only a few bars, he stopped and his hand went out and down Andrew's arm.

"How the divil can anyone put anything in the hat when you hold it that way?" he said. "Hold it out!"

"I'm sorry," said Andrew. "I didn't understand."

"Didn't you? How do you think I live? Or do you consider it beneath you to take money?"

"No."

"Then hold it out!"

He began playing again, and Andrew stood beside him, holding the hat out. A well-dressed lady and a girl of about six approached. The woman glanced at them, and Andrew drew back a little, embarrassed. The woman opened her purse, took out a coin and dropped it into the hat.

"Thank you, madam," said Ben.

He continued playing, and when a gentleman in a white topper dropped sixpence in the hat and Andrew said, "Thank you, sir," Ben smiled faintly.

After playing for some time, he said, "How much have we got?"

"One and nine."

Nodding, Ben tucked the fiddle and bow under his arm, took back his hat and stick and started up Orchard Street toward Baker Street. Though he had not been here for some time, this was familiar ground to Andrew. When they had crossed York Street—Ben waiting at the curb now for Andrew to tell him it was safe—Ben said, "Are we near the Bazaar?"

"Yes, sir. I mean, Ben."

Moving in toward the Bazaar entrance, Ben handed Andrew his hat and stick and again began playing. They did even better here than they had on the corner of Orchard Street—almost half of the passersby dropped something in the hat. They had been there for about twenty minutes when a policeman, walking on the other side of the street, saw them. He hesitated, then began crossing over. At the same time, the door of 221B opened and the heavyset man with military mustache whom Andrew had seen with Sherlock Holmes came out.

"Now then," said the policeman. "You'll have to move along."

"But why, officer?" said the heavyset man. "He's not doing any harm."

"Well, he's obstructing traffic here, sir. But if he moved out toward the curb there'd be no objection to his staying."

"I'll do that, officer," said Ben. And putting his hand on Andrew's shoulder, he started toward the curb.

"Just a second," said the heavyset man, looking at him sympathetically. He took a shilling from his pocket and dropped it into the hat.

"Thank you, sir," said Ben. "God bless you."

He paused when he reached the curb and, for some reason, he was smiling again.

"From now on we won't do so well here," he said to Andrew. "Let's cross."

Andrew guided him across the street, and they took up a new position near the shop that had interested Andrew so much the day he had arrived: Jonathan Walker's. Despite the scowls of a ragged beggar who clearly felt they were invading his territory, they remained there until almost noon. A tall, bearded gentleman wearing a shiny top hat came out of the shop about then, glanced at them casually, and then boarded a brown-and-white bus lettered VICTORIA AND ST. JOHN'S WOOD.

They left shortly after that, went back to Oxford Street where they had sandwiches at a coffee stall, and then worked their way east, stopping at various points along the way. Ben said very little during the afternoon, and Andrew marvelled at the fact that he always seemed to know exactly where he was—which made it possible for him to get about London without any help except when he was crossing streets.

They were in Soho Square when it began to get dark. Ben had been playing music hall tunes and light opera here, for he seemed to know, not only where he was, but what sort of music would appeal most to the passersby in each particular place. He finished "I'm Called Little Buttercup," with a flourish, reached for his hat and stick and said, "We'll go home now."

Tap-tapping with his stick, he led the way out to Oxford Street again. On the far side of Tottenham Court Road was a large building with four tall smokestacks. The sign over the entrance to it read: MEUX'S BREWERY. Further to the right was a lovely church with an old gateway in front of it. Andrew was wondering which of London's many churches it was when Ben said, "St. Giles in the Fields."

Andrew started.

"How did you know what I was thinking?" he asked.

"You don't need eyes for that. Most people with eyes don't really see. I can't see, but I observe. I could tell what you were looking at by the way you turned, and the rest was obvious. Can we cross now?"

"Not yet," said Andrew. A red bus with an advertisement for Okeley's Knife Polish on its modesty board was drawing up in front of them. When it had gone, he said, "Now," and they started across the street.

"Do you know who Hogarth was?" asked Ben abruptly.

"I think so."

"Who?"

"An eighteenth-century painter and engraver. He did *The Rake's Progress*."

"Sure now," said Ben with a faintly mocking note in his voice, "there must be good schools in Cornwall—better than there are in Ireland."

Andrew did not respond.

"Well, it doesn't matter," Ben went on. "Hogarth did quite a few of his slum drawings where we're going. And bad as it was then, you'll find it's not much better now."

They turned right into a narrow street and then into an alley. Even after Ben's warning, Andrew was not prepared for what he saw. The neighborhood in which the Wigginses lived had been poor, crowded, and not too clean, but it was nothing like this. The alley was ankle deep in garbage and filth, which smelled so vile it was hard to breathe. The houses on both sides were so old and dilapidated that it did not seem possible that they could still be standing. Most of them had no windows, and the few doors that remained hung crazily from broken hinges.

Andrew stopped, for the alley was pitch dark. But Ben went ahead, tapping the walls on either side of him with his stick, and Andrew followed. The alley curved and twisted and even narrower passages branched off it. Finally they came into a courtyard lit by a single flaring gas jet. The houses that surrounded the court were as old, distempered and soot-streaked as the ones that lined the alley, but most of them had gin shops or low, candlelit drinking dives on their street floors or in their cellars.

Ben led the way across the court, past a rusty water pump and a fish and chips shop to a house on the far side. He went in, up a flight of rickety stairs with no bannister, unlocked a door and pushed it open. Inside he fumbled in his pocket, took out a box of vestas, struck one and lit a candle that was thrust into the neck of a bottle.

Andrew stood in the doorway, looking around. The

room was bare except for two mattresses that lay on the floor and a cracked pitcher.

"Well, here we are," said Ben. If he was aware of Andrew's dismay, he gave no sign of it. "Are you hungry?"

"Yes."

"Here." He took out some of the money they had collected and held it out. "Get us some fish and chips."

"Yes, sir. I mean, Ben."

He went down the stairs again slowly, feeling lonely, miserable, and anxious. He had lost his fear of London—of the unknown and frightening world it represented—during the time he had been staying with the Wigginses. But now, in this strange place, surrounded by squalor and depravity, and cut off from all contact with anyone he really knew, it all came flooding back again, and he bitterly regretted saying he would go with the blind Irishman.

Voices—shouts, curses and snatches of song—came from the dives and grog shops that surrounded the court. Dark shapes huddled in the doorways or lurked in the passages that led into the yard, and he was conscious of eyes—many and unfriendly eyes—watching him. He tried to ignore them as he walked toward the fish and chips shop. He was just a few steps from the door when a figure came out of the shadows and stopped in front of him; a boy who was probably fifteen. His cropped hair stood up in bristles, his face was streaked with dirt, and he looked at Andrew with open dislike.

"Oo's yer?" he said with so thick a Cockney accent that Andrew could hardly understand him.

"Andrew."

"Wotcha doing here?"

"I'm with Ben, the blind man."

The boy continued looking at him, his small, blue eyes as hard as pebbles. His lips moved. Andrew knew what was coming and, as the boy spat at him, he stepped aside and hurried into the shop.

This was all familiar. He had been through it before in Gorlyn. Grownups, who should know better, were always making you do something you did not want to do and then leaving you to face the consequences alone: the hostility of those your own age who resented you because you were different.

He asked for two orders of fish and chips, was handed them in cones of newspapers, paid for them and looked out. There was no sign of the boy. But, as he left the shop, there he was again, waiting in the shadows to the side of the door.

"Gimme those," he said, reaching for the fish and chips.

"What?"

"Give 'em to me or I'll smash your gob!"

Rage kindled in Andrew's stomach, flared upward. Yes, he'd been through it all before, and there was only one answer to it.

Two men and a woman had come out of a nearby gin shop and were standing there a little unsteadily, watching. The woman, in a bedraggled feathered hat, must have been pretty when she was young. She was no longer young now—her face was powdered and painted—but her eyes were not unfriendly.

Andrew brushed past the boy.

"Excuse me, ma'am," he said, "but would you hold these for me?"

One of the men guffawed. "Ma'am!" he said. "Listen to him!"

"Shut up!" said the woman fiercely. "Just because he treats me like a lady . . . Are you gonna fight him?" she asked Andrew.

"Yes."

"It's young Danny," she said. "He's a bad 'un, but . . . Yes, I'll hold them." She took the two papers of fish and chips. "And good luck to you."

"Thanks."

He turned back to face the boy, who stared at him for a moment, then, grinning, came at him with swinging fists.

Rage still gripped Andrew. From the beginning—
when the trouble had first started in Cornwall—his
sense of outrage had made him willing to take any
amount of punishment in a fight if he could return it.
But one of the things Trefethen had taught him, along
with everything else, was to control his anger.

The boy, Danny, was no boxer. His blows were wide
and wild, and Andrew had little difficulty ducking or
blocking them. But he knew that if one of them landed,
he was finished. He kept jabbing to keep Danny off
balance, side-stepping when he rushed him, and was
hoping to tire him out. Then, suddenly, one of Andrew's feet slipped in the mud of the courtyard, and he
went down.

With a shout, Danny leaped forward, swung a heavy
boot and kicked him in the side and in the thigh. When
he drew his foot back to kick him again in the head,
Andrew rolled over and away, got to his feet. He was
so furious that he felt no pain. Even in a free-for-all,
you didn't kick someone when he was down. He set
himself and, when Danny came charging in to finish
him, he drove a hard left to his stomach and a right to
his face.

Danny staggered back, blood dripping from his nose
and a look of surprise on his face. Then, as he came on
again, Andrew half turned and, catching him by one
arm, tossed him with a hip throw. Danny landed heavily and lay on the ground half stunned.

A roar went up from the crowd that had gathered to
watch.

"You've got him now!" someone shouted. "Bash
him!"

Andrew went over to Danny, waited till he had struggled to one knee.

"Had enough?" he asked.

Danny looked at him dully.

"I said, have you had enough?"

Slowly Danny nodded.

"All right, then."

He glanced around. The woman who was holding the fish and chips came toward him.

"That was ream!" she said, her eyes shining. "You're a young wonder, you are."

"Fights like a tiger," said one of the men with her.

"Thanks," said Andrew. "And thanks for holding those for me."

"No need to thank me," she said. "But watch out for that Danny. He'll try and nobble you again sometime."

"I expect he will," said Andrew. "Thanks again." And taking the fish and chips, he went across the yard and into the house. By the time he had climbed the stairs, his side ached and his leg hurt so much that he had trouble walking.

"Andrew?" said Ben when he opened the door.

"Yes."

"What was that noise out there? A fight?"

"Yes."

"There are a dozen a night. Wait a minute." He listened as Andrew came toward him. "You're limping. Were you in it?"

"Yes."

"What happened?"

He stood there quietly as Andrew told him, then chuckled.

"You finished him with a hip throw?"

"Yes."

"Where'd you learn to fight like that?"

"From a blacksmith in Cornwall. He'd been county champion."

"Not Marquis of Queensberry, I take it."

"No. Old style—bare fists."

Ben nodded. "That's where the throw came in—very useful in a free-for-all. How badly are you hurt?"

"Not too badly. Just my leg and side where he kicked me."

"I shouldn't have sent you down there alone. I won't do it again." He smiled grimly. "You've had quite an education—Hogarth and catch-as-catch-can fighting. Shall we eat?"

Andrew handed him one of the paper cones, and they ate in silence.

"There's something we'd better talk about," said Ben when they were finished. "How long have you been in London?"

"About ten days."

"No, you haven't. You just got here yesterday, and you don't know anyone. Not Wiggins, not anyone. We met in Penzance about two weeks ago, and you've been with me ever since. Do you understand?"

"Yes."

"Good." He lifted a loose floor board, took out two blankets, and gave one to Andrew. "It been a long day, and you must be tired," he said. "We'll go to sleep now."

"All right."

"I hope your leg and side won't bother you too much."

"Thank you."

Andrew stretched out on the mattress and covered himself with the blanket. He *was* tired. The mattress was lumpy and his leg and side ached, but neither of those things bothered him as much as the cold, for there was no glass in the windows and a chilly breeze blew through the room. In spite of that, he fell asleep. He woke once, sometime during the night, feeling warmer, more comfortable. He reached down and discovered the reason for it. Ben had thrown his cloak over him so that he was covered with that as well as the blanket.

9

Broken Nose Reappears

When Andrew first woke the next morning, his side hurt and his leg was stiff. But getting up and moving about seemed to help, and by the time he had gone down to the pump in the courtyard, filled the pitcher and brought it back to the room, he felt much better.

He and Ben washed rather sketchily, hid the blankets under the floor boards, then locked up and went down the stairs together. There was no one in the courtyard when they left the rookery. They had tea and buns at a stall in Soho, then began a round that was similar to the one they had followed the day before. This time, however, Ben was even more silent than he had been and, when he was not playing the fiddle, Andrew had the feeling that he was listening intently to everything that was said around them.

They had meat pies in Covent Garden for supper and returned to St. Giles just as it was getting dark. By now the courtyard and the rookery that surrounded it had become the place that Hogarth had drawn and painted: a self-contained night world that was noisy, garish and vibrant with life. Lights burned in the gin shops, and standing in front of one of them was the boy, Danny. When he saw Andrew, he whistled softly, and a burly man in soiled but flashy clothes came out of one of the gin shops. Danny jerked his head at Andrew, and the two of them advanced toward him.

"Why are you stopping?" asked Ben.

"That boy I fought last night. There's a man with him, and they're coming this way."

"Ah," said Ben. "Hold my fiddle." He handed it to Andrew. "And what are you after?" he asked the burly man.

"Your nipper," said the man. "He bashed my brother."

"In a fair fight," said Ben.

"Fair or not, I'm going to teach him a lesson."

"You're not," said Ben.

The man looked at him in surprise, then laughed.

"Don't be daft," he said. "Out of the way. I don't want to hurt you."

"And you won't," said Ben quietly.

Again the man looked at him. Then, as he raised a hand to push him aside Ben—shortening his grip on his stick—drove the end of it just under his ribs. The man doubled up, gasping.

"You sod!" he said when he had straightened up. "I'll nobble you proper!"

Reaching into a back pocket, he pulled out a blackjack.

"No!" said Andrew, jumping in front of Ben. "Can't you see that he's blind? You can't . . ."

The man cuffed him, knocking him down. But, as he raised the blackjack, Ben swung his stick in a full-armed slash, striking the man across the knuckles and knocking the blackjack out of his hand. With a howl, the man staggered back, clutching his hand. Recovering, he bent down to pick up the cosh, but again, by sound or by instinct, Ben seemed to know exactly what the man was doing, and the stick shot out, pausing an inch from his face.

"Leave it," he said.

"What?"

"I said, leave it."

Slowly the man straightened up, staring at Ben, who, grey-haired and sightless, had acted with a speed and decisiveness that were somehow frightening; much more frightening than if he had been young and had all his faculties.

"I may be blind," said Ben quietly, "but blind or not, I'm a match for you or any three like you. So don't be trying it on again either with me or the boy."

The man looked at him for a moment longer, then leaving the blackjack on the ground, he walked off, followed by Danny.

"Are you all right?" asked Ben as Andrew got to his feet.

"Yes, Ben."

"And the fiddle?"

Andrew had dropped it when he fell. Now he examined it.

"All right too."

"Come then." And, tapping with his stick, he led the way through the awed and wondering crowd. When they were in the room, Ben took the fiddle from Andrew, ran his fingers over it, played a few notes and, satisfied, put it down.

"I don't think he or the boy will bother you again," he said.

"I don't either."

"It's been a long day, but there's something I must do later. Are you up to it or are you too tired?"

Andrew studied him. Apart fom his aunt, there had been few people during his entire life who had shown any real interest in him, ever given him help or comfort; only Jack Trefethen in Cornwall and more recently the Wigginses, particularly Screamer. But though they had been his friends, none of them—no one ever—had protected him, fought for him, as Ben had. He was a strange man, and Andrew still did not understand him, but there was no question as to how he felt about him.

"I'm not too tired," he said.

"Good. Stretch out and rest then, and I'll call you when it's time."

It was probably around eleven o'clock—Andrew had been dozing and was not sure of the time—when Ben shook him gently. He got up, and they went down to

93

the courtyard. Andrew had expected that they would leave the rookery but Ben tapped his way to one of the gin shops and pushed open the door.

The room inside was large, low-ceilinged, and lit by candles. It was quite crowded and noisy, and the air was thick with tobacco smoke. The babble of voices—mostly Irish it seemed to Andrew—died as they entered.

"Is there a table?" asked Ben.

"Yes. Over there," said Andrew, moving toward one in the far corner.

"Who is he?" asked someone as they sat down on a bench against the wall.

"The blind fiddler that did down Big Danny, the rampsman."

"Ah," said the first man, a navvy in rough, work-stained clothes. "What's your name?" he asked.

"Ben."

"And where are you from?"

"Sure and if you're Irish yourself, you should know that."

"How would I know it?"

"How do I know you're from Shannon?"

The navvy raised an eyebrow. "You've sharp ears," he said. "You're right."

"And I," said the man with him, "where am I from?"

"From Cork."

"Right again. You should be in a music hall."

"I'd rather be here," said Ben.

This drew a chuckle from those who were listening, but the navvy persisted.

"Say something else, and let's see if I can place where you're from."

"*Pogue ma hone!*" said Ben.

Andrew did not know what that meant, but it must have been at least mildly insulting for it raised, not just a chuckle, but a laugh, and the navvy grinned.

"You're all right, old man," he said. "And with a tongue like that I'd say you were from Sligo."

"That's close enough," said Ben.

"Will you take something, then?"

"I'm not here for the fresh sea air."

The navvy nodded to the man behind the bar, and he brought Ben a glass of hot gin with a slice of lemon in it.

"*Slainte*," said Ben, raising his glass. There was a murmured response.

"I see you've your fiddle with you," said the man from Cork. "Would you play us something?"

"For company like this, it'd be a pleasure," said Ben. He took another sip of the hot gin, then tucked the fiddle under his chin and began to play. As far as Andrew could tell, everything he played was Irish; sometimes quick dance tunes like reels or jigs, sometimes slow and mournful ones and sometimes lilting ballads. When he stopped, there was stamping of feet and applause, and the man from Cork bought him another gin.

They sat there for some time, Ben drinking his gin slowly and, when he had finished it, leaning back with his head against the wall. He looked as if he were asleep, but Andrew had the feeling that he wasn't; that he was listening to the conversations that were going on around him as he had listened during the day in the streets. He wondered how long they were going to stay there, for while Ben may only have been pretending, Andrew himself was starting to get sleepy.

The door opened and closed as it had several times before, and Andrew glanced casually through the smoky half-darkness, then stiffened. This time the man who had come in was the cab driver with the broken nose who had taken Mr. Dennison away in the growler and chased and almost caught Andrew.

Ben, as always, either felt or sensed his movement. "What is it?" he asked quietly.

"Someone I know just came in."

"Who?"

"A cab driver."

"And you're afraid of him."

"Yes."

"Why?"

"It's a long story."

"Save it till later then, but watch him."

Broken Nose pushed his way to the zinc-covered bar, bought himself a drink, then turned and looked over the noisy company. He glanced at Ben, at Andrew, then sat down facing the door. If he had recognized Andrew with his head cropped and in his old, badly fitting clothes, he gave no indication of it.

"What's he doing?" asked Ben.

"Sitting there. He seems to be waiting for someone."

Ben nodded. About fifteen minutes later the door opened again, but this time the man who came in and stood there looking around was someone quite different. He was young and slim and quite well dressed. His eyes met those of the broken-nosed cabby, then he turned and went out again. Almost immediately Broken Nose got up and went out also.

"He's going," whispered Andrew.

Again Ben nodded. Sitting up, he yawned, stretched, then rose and said, "Good night to you all."

He put his hand on Andrew's shoulder and let him lead the way to the door. When they got outside, Broken Nose was just disappearing into the alley.

"Follow him," said Ben. "But not too closely."

He put his hand on Andrew's shoulder so he would not have to use his stick, and they went out through the alley. Broken Nose had turned left and was walking toward New Oxford Street. When he had crossed it, they hurried after him. About fifty feet further on, he turned left again into another alley. When they reached it, Andrew saw that it was almost as narrow as the one that led into the rookery. There was no sign of either the slim young man or Broken Nose, but the door of a large building that seemed to be an abandoned warehouse was just closing.

"He's gone into a big, old building," said Andrew. "I think it's a warehouse."

"Hold these," said Ben, handing over his fiddle and stick. "And wait here."

His hand on the wall of the building, Ben went quietly down the alley, paused when he got to the warehouse door, put his ear to it and listened. Apparently he could not hear anything, for after a moment he went on and listened at a boarded up window. He remained there for some time, but apparently he could not hear anything there either for, with an impatient gesture, he turned and came back to where Andrew was waiting.

"We'll go back to the room now," he said.

They returned to the rookery in silence, and when they were in the room and Ben had lit the candle, he said, "Tell me about the man you were afraid of."

He listened while Andrew told him of his two encounters with the broken-nosed cabby.

"You said Mr. Dennison was a master at the local school?"

"Yes."

"You only knew him there?"

"No. About two years ago my aunt made arrangements for him to teach me privately—tutor me. I didn't like the idea—I knew there'd be trouble—but she insisted."

"What do you mean by trouble?"

"With the other boys in Gorlyn."

"Of course. In a village like that they'd resent your doing anything different from what they did. I take it that Dennison was a university man."

"Yes. I believe he was at Oxford."

"And he was tutoring you so that you could get into one of the good public schools."

"I think so."

"Did he know London?"

"He seemed to."

"Was he a good friend of your aunt's?"

"No. At least, not at first. He used to ask me questions about her and also about my parents—who they were. But I couldn't answer because I don't really know much about them. Then, when Aunt Agnes became ill, he began going to see her, talking to her."

"About what?"

"I don't know, but I had the feeling that Aunt Agnes didn't like it very much."

"And after she died, he took you in, took care of you?"

"Yes. I didn't want to live with him, but there was no one else and Aunt Agnes told me I should—for a while at least."

"Ah! You say you know nothing about your parents?"

"No. Aunt Agnes once told me that my father was a gentleman, but that was all."

"What about your mother? Didn't you ever see her, get any letters from her?"

Andrew hesitated. He had never talked about his mother to anyone except his aunt, and he didn't know why Ben was so interested in her, but since he clearly was . . .

"No. I never got any letters from her, though I think Aunt Agnes did. But I remember her."

"She came to see you at Gorlyn?"

"Yes. Twice. Once when I was very small and once when I was about four. I remember that she was very beautiful—she wore a big hat—and she hugged me and kissed me and cried and said that one day we'd be together for good and then she went away again."

"And you haven't seen her since?" Ben's voice was surprisingly gentle.

"No."

"Well, who knows? One day you may."

He took the blankets from under the floor boards, gave one to Andrew and said, "It's late and you must be tired. Go to sleep now."

"I will. Goodnight, Ben."

"Goodnight."

Andrew stretched out on the mattress and covered himself with the blanket. Ben remained where he was, sitting with his back to the wall. He seemed to be thinking—Andrew did not know about what—but somehow he did not feel as cold as he had the night before. Not only that, but for some reason—possibly because he had talked about things he had never talked about to anyone before—he felt less anxious and more hopeful than he had since his aunt died.

10

The Listener

"Do you trust me, Andrew?"

Andrew looked at the blind fiddler with surprise. He must know the answer to that, must know how Andrew felt about him, especially after everything that had happened the day before. But since he seemed to want a response, Andrew said, "Yes, Ben."

"Good. We're going to do something that will seem odd to you, but I want you to do exactly what I tell you, and do it without asking any questions."

"All right, Ben."

They were standing in front of the Bazaar on Baker Street. Since it had been very late when they got to sleep, they had not gotten up as early as usual that morning. By the time they had had their breakfast at a coffee stall, it was a little after ten. Ben had played for a while in Soho, then they had walked west to Baker Street.

Ben told him what he wanted to do and, though it certainly was rather strange, Andrew did not comment. Ben tucked his fiddle under his chin and began to play again, and Andrew, holding the wide brimmed black hat, stood beside him looking up the street.

A few minutes after eleven, the heavyset man with the military mustache came out of 221B. He was wearing a top hat and carrying a small black bag as Ben had said he would.

"He's coming," said Andrew quietly.

Ben continued playing. Then, as the man came towards them, he lowered his fiddle and stepped forward, bumping into the man and knocking off his hat. Andrew, who had circled behind them, caught it. Tucked inside the hat was a stethoscope. Whipping it out, he hid it in his jacket, passed the hat to Ben, and hurried off up the street.

Behind him he heard Ben saying, "I beg your pardon, sir. I hope I didn't hurt you."

"Not at all," said the man.

Glancing back, Andrew saw Ben give the man his hat. He put it on without looking inside it, continued on to the curb, and waved to a hansom. Andrew paused, waiting for Ben to catch up with him.

"Did you get it?" asked Ben.

"Yes. He never noticed it was gone so I didn't run."

"Good lad. We'll get it back to him one of these days." And smiling as he had the day the man gave him a shilling, he let Andrew lead him back down Baker Street and then east.

When they got to Picadilly, a newsboy, papers under his arm, ran past them calling, "Dynamiters strike again!" and Ben paused abruptly.

"Boy!" he called.

He bought a paper and gave it to Andrew.

"Tell me where the dynamiting was," he said.

Andrew skimmed the article, which took up most of the first column.

"On Pall Mall, near one of the clubs."

"Anyone hurt?"

"No. Some windows were broken, but that's all."

"Ah," said Ben. "Let's have lunch."

They spent most of the afternoon around Leicester Square and in Soho and had dinner in a rather grubby restaurant near Seven Dials. Ben was strangely silent, as he had been most of the day, and when they had finished dinner, he said, "We've some more business to take care of tonight. We'd better go back to St. Giles."

When they were in the room, Ben said, "Stand at the window and tell me if you can see that gin shop we were in last night."

Andrew looked out. He found he could see about

half of the courtyard, including the door of the gin shop.

"Yes, I can."

"Well, keep your eye on it and tell me if you see your cabby with the broken nose."

Andrew pulled his mattress over and sat down on it. During the next hour or so, he watched the courtyard come to life as it always did after dark; children played under the flaring gas jet, women with shawls went to the rusty pump to get water, and flashily-dressed men and women came down the alley and went into the various gin shops. Finally:

"There he is," he said.

"Did he go in?"

"Yes."

"Well, tell me when he leaves."

Again they had to wait, but at last the cabby came out and stood there for a moment, looking around.

"He just came out."

"We'll go then. No need to hurry. We know where he's going."

They went down and out through the alley. When they reached the street, the cabby was just crossing New Oxford Street. They waited until he had turned into the passage that led to the old warehouse, then followed. Again Ben told Andrew to wait while he went down the passage. Taking the stethoscope from his pocket, he put the earpieces in his ears, pressed the other end to the boarded-up window. He remained there for several minutes, listening, and from the expression on his face, Andrew knew that now he could hear what was going on inside. Abruptly he straightened up and came out.

"This way," he said. "Quickly."

They walked north, away from St. Giles. Then, when they heard the warehouse door open and close, they turned around and walked back as if they were returning to the rookery. Broken Nose was just coming out of the passage when they reached it. He looked at them sharply, and turned right.

Ben took a watch from his pocket, pressed a button, and it chimed softly nine times, then three more times.

"Quarter of ten," he said. "We may be able to make it. Let's find a cab."

They went west. A hansom was standing in front of the Oxford Music Hall at St. Giles Circus, and Ben hailed it.

"The General Post Office," he said.

"It closes at ten," said the cabby.

"I know. You've ten minutes to make it, and there's ten bob for yourself if you do."

"Get in," said the cabby.

They got in. The cabby cracked his whip, and they were off. Andrew had wanted to ride in a hansom ever since he came to London, and he settled back to enjoy it. Lighter and more maneuverable than a growler, the hansom travelled more quickly, rocking and swaying but running smoothly on its rubber-tired wheels. Urged on by the cabby, the horse moved on at a steady trot, sometimes breaking into a gallop. They went along High Holborn, over the Holborn Viaduct and up Newgate Street where they turned left and stopped in front of an imposing building.

"Did it," said the cabby.

"Good man," said Ben.

He paid him, and the cabby touched his billycock hat with his whip. They hurried to the door of the Post Office.

"Hold this and wait here," said Ben, giving Andrew his fiddle. "I won't be long."

Tapping with his stick, he went in alone and over to the telegraph window. He came out in a few minutes, smiling quietly and more relaxed than Andrew had ever seen him.

"It's a long walk back," he said. "Let's take a bus."

They hailed one on the corner of Newgate Street, climbed to the top deck and rode back the way they had come.

"Are we going out again?" asked Andrew when they were once more in the bare, drafty room.

"No," said Ben. "Are you tired?"

"A little."

"Well, it's been a long day. But you'll have a chance to rest up now. Tomorrow you can go back to the Wigginses."

"Go back?"

"Yes. I won't be needing you anymore. At least, not to lead me."

"Oh," said Andrew, disappointed. "Then I won't be seeing you again?"

Ben turned toward him.

"I wouldn't say that. Does it matter?"

"Yes."

"Why?" Andrew did not answer. "I suspect that one way or another we will see one another. We'll talk about it in the morning. But it's late and you'd better go to sleep now."

They took the blankets from under the floor boards, and Andrew stretched out on the mattress and covered himself.

"Goodnight, Andrew," said Ben.

"Goodnight, Mr. Holmes," said Andrew.

Ben stiffened.

"What did you say?" he asked.

"I'm sorry. I meant . . . goodnight, Ben."

"But you said Mr. Holmes."

"Yes."

"So you guessed who I was."

"Yes."

"How?"

"Well, Sam said the job he knew about didn't have anything to do with you, but I wondered—I guess because I *wanted* it to have something to do with you. And it seemed to me that if you were in disguise you wouldn't be able to have Sam or one of the regular Irregulars with you because too many people know them."

"That's why I asked Sam if he knew of anyone else. But there must have been more to it than that."

"There was the way you acted, some of the things you did."

"For instance?"

"Well, you were always so sure of yourself, knew just what you were doing. But I guess the most important thing was the way you smiled the two times we saw the man with the mustache in front of your house on Baker Street."

"My friend, Dr. Watson. Sam said you were bright, Andrew, and you are. What's more, you're observant. But what about my eyes?"

"That's the one thing I couldn't understand. But I decided it must be some kind of a trick."

"There's more to evidence than there appears to be," said Holmes, nodding. "There are subjective factors that can outweigh the objective ones. You've got the makings of good detective, Andrew. As for the trick . . . here."

Pulling carefully and delicately at one of his blank, blind eyes, he removed it and held it out to Andrew.

"I had it made out of gutta percha," he said. "The inner part fits between the cornea and the eyelids. The outer part covers my eyes. And there's a tiny, almost invisible hole in it so I can see—not well—but a little."

"I never would have known it."

"I hope no one else did. I don't think anyone did—not even Watson. Yes, you're quite an unusual boy, Andrew. And since we've at least one piece of unfinished business, you certainly will be seeing me again."

11

The Bomb Squad

Mr. Victor Lucas, manager of Christie and Manson's Auction Rooms, was having a busy morning. Besides the sale that was to take place that afternoon—an extensive and complicated one—he was also supervising the hanging of an exhibition of paintings that were to go on the block in two days. And since the paintings included four very important ones that were being sold for the new Lord Lowther, he was being particularly careful about their arrangement.

Deciding that the Lowther paintings should go on the large wall opposite the window, with the Reynolds and the Constable in the center, he gave the necessary orders and went out to the entrance hall. Two porters in their long, striped aprons were standing there looking at a large crate.

"What's this?" he asked.

"Don't know, sir," said one of the porters. "Two delivery men just brought it in."

"But they shouldn't have brought it in here. Why didn't they take it to the service entrance?"

"I told them to," said the porter. "But they just made some unpleasant remarks, put it down and left."

"I wish you'd called me," said Mr. Lucas, irritated. "I'd have had something unpleasant to say to them. I'm sick of people not doing what they're supposed to."

He examined the label on the crate. It had been shipped to Christie and Manson by D. B. Cox of Redcliffe Crescent, Bristol.

"Cox," he said. "I remember. Rugs and tapestries

sent here for appraisal and possible sale. Take it down to the store room, and I'll have it opened later."

"Yes, Mr. Lucas," said the porter.

He and his mate advanced on the crate and were preparing to lift it when the door opened and a stocky, aggressive looking man in a bowler strode in followed by two policemen.

"Where will I find the manager?" he asked brusquely.

"I'm the manager," said Lucas rather stiffly.

"Name?"

"Victor Lucas."

"I'm Inspector Leggett of the Bomb Squad."

"Bomb Squad?"

"Yes. Scotland Yard. We've just received confidential but reliable information that an attempt may be made to bomb your establishment sometime today."

"What? You're not serious, Inspector!"

Leggett looked at him coldly. "I don't have the time, nor is it my habit, to indulge in practical jokes. I assume you read the papers."

"You're referring to the bombing in Pall Mall the day before yesterday?"

"*And* to the one in the Baker Street Underground. And two attempts you don't know about."

Lucas looked around anxiously. "But what do we do about it? We're holding an auction this afternoon."

"You may have to call it off. But first we'll search the premises."

He jerked his head and the two policemen approached.

"Start at the bottom," he said. "Cellar, store rooms, and work your way up. I'll cover this floor here."

As the policemen saluted and started to move off, Leggett glanced at the crate.

"What's this?" he asked.

"It just arrived," said Lucas. "Rugs and tapestries, I believe."

Leggett bent down to read the address on the label, then stiffened and leaned closer to the crate.

"Come here and listen," he said to Lucas.

Nervously the manager bent down also, pressing his ear to the crate. From somewhere deep inside it he heard a quiet but ominous ticking.

"Oh, no!" he said. "You don't mean . . . ?"

"Out!" ordered Leggett. "Everyone out! Clear the building!"

"But . . ."

"I said, out! Jones," he said to one of the two policemen, "get those people out!" He nodded toward the exhibition room where two of Mr. Lucas's assistants were looking out at him anxiously. "Simmons, clear the rest of the building!"

As the policemen moved off, the assistants joined Mr. Lucas, and all three of them hurried out into King Street. In front of the door was a solidly built wooden van covered with steel mesh. Bold red letters on its side said: DANGER. BOMB DISPOSAL UNIT. The uniformed driver, a heavyset man with a crooked nose, looked down at them impassively, then glanced at the open door.

The rest of Mr. Lucas's staff began coming out of the building: auctioneers and clerks, appraisers, porters, carpenters. They stood in a hushed group around the manager, watching the open door like the driver of the van.

Then Leggett appeared. The two policemen were behind him, carrying the crate.

"Open up, Barney," called Leggett.

The driver jumped down from the box, went around to the rear of the van and opened the door.

"Careful now," said Leggett as the policemen came down the steps with the crate. Then to Lucas, "We're not going to try and open it here. We're taking it to the proving grounds."

The two policemen eased the crate into the rear of the van, closed and locked the door, then climbed up to the high front seat where they were joined by the driver and Leggett.

"I assume you'll let me know . . ." began Lucas.

109

Leggett nodded grimly.

"All right, Barney," he said. "Drive like the devil!"

The driver cracked his whip, the horses broke into a trot, and the van rumbled off up King Street, turned left on Duke Street.

A sigh went up from the crowd in front of the auction rooms.

"I must say, you have to be pretty brave to do that sort of thing," said one of Mr. Lucas's assistants.

"Brave?" said the other. "You wouldn't catch me doing it for a thousand pounds!"

"All right, all right. Back inside all of you," said Mr. Lucas impatiently. "We've got work to do."

It was shortly after this that Dr. Watson heard a hansom stop in front of 221B. Looking out, he saw Holmes paying the driver. He went to the door and had it open as Holmes came up the stairs carrying his bag.

"It's good to see you, Holmes," he said, shaking his hand. "I had no idea when you were coming back."

"Neither had I," said Holmes.

"How was Paris?"

"I suspect much as it always was."

"You suspect?" He studied his friend. "Was your trip successful?"

"I don't know yet. Has Inspector Gregory been here?"

"No."

Holmes glanced at his watch.

"It's still early. He should be here in an hour or so. How have you been, Watson?"

"Well enough. Have you had lunch?"

"No. And I'm famished."

"Why don't I ring and tell Mrs. Hudson . . ."

"Just a second." Holmes opened his bag. "I have something for you."

"A present?"

"You might call it that. Here." And he handed Watson a stethoscope.

"Holmes, this is truly remarkable!"

"How so?"

"I lost my old stethoscope two days ago—I'm not sure where or how. And for you to have gotten me another . . ." He broke off. "But this is my old one!"

"Yes."

"Where did you get it?"

"From you," said Holmes, smiling.

"What?"

"But . . ." Watson eyes widened. "The blind Irish fiddler who bumped into me, knocked off my hat . . ."

"Yes, Watson. One of my better disguises. I needed the stethoscope, hoped you wouldn't mind my borrowing it for a day or so."

"Then you never went to Paris?"

"No. It was important that I pretend I had, but I was here the whole time."

"But . . ."

"I really am famished, Watson. I've been living on food that was barely edible since I left here. Let's have Mrs. Hudson up, order a really special lunch, and when Gregory gets here, I'll explain."

They had finished lunch, a quite lavish one, and Holmes was filling his pipe when Gregory arrived.

"I got your telegram, Holmes," he said. "How was your trip?"

"Interesting. How have things been here?"

"Fairly quiet."

"No more bombings?"

"There was one—not very serious—in Pall Mall the other day."

"Yes, I know about that. Nothing else? Nothing strange or unusual happened today?"

"Now that you mention it, there was something. I planned to look into it later on. Just before I left the Yard, we got a note from a Mr. Lucas, manager of Christie and Manson's, thanking us for our prompt and courageous action in removing a bomb from their premises."

"Removing a bomb?"

"Yes. Which puzzled us a bit. Because, while we do have a bomb squad, they had not been there."

"I see. Any more details in his note?"

"No. Except that he wanted to know if we felt it was safe for them to go ahead with their plans for an important sale they were holding the day after tomorrow."

"If I'm not mistaken, that's the one at which Lytell's paintings will be put up."

"Lytell?"

"The new Lord Lowther. That's very interesting." Getting up, Holmes walked to the window and stood there for a moment puffing on his pipe. "Have there been any strange deaths or disappearances since I went away?"

"Just the usual ones. Nothing particularly strange."

"Any that involved an artist?"

"What?" Gregory looked at him in surprise.

"There was one. Nothing to do with my branch, though I believe the Arson Squad is looking into it. There was a bad fire in Chelsea, and a painter named Follette was burned to death in his studio."

"Oh?" Holmes turned from the window. "You said you were planning to go to Christie and Manson's?"

"I thought I might stop by and talk to this Mr. Lucas."

"I think you should, Gregory. I want to talk to someone myself and send a telegram, but Watson and I will meet you at Christie's at four o'clock."

Holmes glanced at his companion as they got out of the hansom on King Street.

"You've been unusually quiet, Watson," he said.

"Puzzled would be more accurate. I don't understand any of this."

"I'm not surprised. But be patient. Once I've made certain of one or two things, I'll be glad to explain. After all," he smiled a faintly ironic smile, "it would be very shortsighted of me to keep my Boswell in the dark."

"It always seemed to me that Johnson was more appreciative of Boswell's efforts than you've been of mine. However . . ." He broke off as a tall man in tweeds rounded the corner and came toward them. "Isn't that your friend, Lytell?"

"Yes. I asked him to meet us here. You're very prompt," he said as Lytell reached them.

"A habit I find hard to break," said Lytell, shaking hands with him and nodding to Watson. "Besides I was curious as to why you wanted me to meet you here of all places."

"Let's go in and perhaps I can satisfy your curiosity."

Inspector Gregory was in the entrance hall talking to a worried looking man in a frock coat.

"Ah, there you are, Holmes," he said. "May I introduce Mr. Lucas, manager of Christie's?"

"Mr. Lucas," said Holmes. "I believe you know Lord Lowther."

"Indeed, yes," said Lucas, bowing. "My lord."

"And this is my friend, Dr. Watson. Lytell, this is Inspector Gregory of Scotland Yard."

"This gets more and more interesting," said Lytell. "Am I to surmise that you brought me here on a police matter?"

"I suspect it may be," said Holmes. "Mr. Lucas, would you tell us exactly what happened this morning when the men from the bomb squad came here?"

"Why, yes, Mr. Holmes."

When he was finished, Holmes nodded.

"Where were Lord Lowther's paintings at the time?" he asked.

"Leaning against the wall there. I had had them brought up from the store room, left them there while I decided where to hang them."

"And where are they now?"

"In here."

He led the way into the exhibition room, pointed to four paintings in the center of the wall opposite the window.

"Those are, in fact, your paintings, Lytell?" asked Holmes.

Lytell glanced at them.

"Yes."

"There's no question about it?"

With a puzzled frown, Lytell looked at him, then approached the paintings and examined each in turn.

"No. None. Why should there be?"

"We're none of us perfect. I could be mistaken," said Holmes. "But . . ." He turned as a dapper man wearing pince-nez came in. "Ah, Mr. Wilson."

"I'm afraid I'm a bit late, Mr. Holmes," said the man with the pince-nez. "Sorry."

"It doesn't matter. Gentlemen, may I present Mr. Derek Wilson of the Tate Gallery?"

"We know one another," said Lucas. "We have called on Mr. Wilson on several occasions to authenticate doubtful paintings."

"Then you would accept him as an authority?"

"Indubitably. I don't believe he has an equal, certainly not as far as English paintings are concerned."

"In that case, Mr. Wilson," said Holmes, "may we have your opinion on these four?"

"Why, yes, Mr. Holmes," said Wilson, walking over to the paintings. "Of course I'm familiar with *Lady Lydia*. I've always considered it one of Sir Joshua's best. And the Constable is one of my favorites. As for the Rubens and the Carvaggio . . ."

He paused, leaning close to the Reynolds, then stepped back again. Frowning, he took a magnifying glass from his pocket and examined the painting carefully, then did the same with the Constable. He moved on to the Rubens and was just turning his attention to the Carvaggio when Holmes said, "Well, Mr. Wilson?"

"Excellent work," said Wilson. "At least the *Lady Lydia* and the Constable are. But clearly copies."

"Copies?" said Lytell.

"But that's impossible!" said Lucas, his face pale. "Are you sure?"

"No question about it," said Wilson. "As I said,

they're very well done, but the brushwork's all wrong. As for the other two, I'd like a little more time to examine them . . ."

"I think we can assume that they're forgeries too," said Holmes. "Which means that you have another case to solve, Gregory. On the other hand, you can reassure the Prime Minister about the bombings. I don't believe there will be any more."

12

Holmes' Strange Advice and Odd Behavior

"I'm afraid I still don't understand it," said Lytell.

"Nor I," said Watson.

They had come back to Baker Street from Christie and Manson's and now, for the first time, Holmes seemed ready to answer their questions.

"Part of it's quite simple," he said. "Gregory had asked me to look into the bombings, and one of the first things that struck me about them was the fact that they had caused surprisingly little damage."

"A ticket taker was injured in the first one," said Watson.

"That, I believe, was an accident. In any case, though, they created a good deal of anxiety—which was their purpose—they could not be compared to the really terrible bombings that took place in the early eighties."

"Agreed," said Watson.

"For reasons I won't go into now, I was convinced that whoever was responsible for the bombings wanted me out of the country, evidently believing that I would be called in to investigate them. So I obliged by pretending to go to Paris. When it appeared that I was gone, the bombings intensified."

"But what did they have to do with the theft of the paintings?" asked Lytell.

"They were the preparation for it. After all the newspaper headlines, when the spurious bomb squad appeared at Christie and Manson's, Lucas was quite prepared to believe that the men were from Scotland Yard. The copies of the paintings were of course in the crate that had supposedly been sent there by Cox of Bristol." He smiled. "Whoever was responsible did show a certain pawky humor there."

"The play, *Cox and Box?*" said Lytell.

"Exactly. When the building was cleared, the thieves opened the crate, took out and left the copies, put the originals in the crate and made off with them."

"And you knew that all the time?" said Watson.

"No. I suspected that the bombings weren't political, as the earlier ones had been, and I confirmed this during the time I was underground, masquerading as a blind fiddler. Because patriots in Irish circles who might have been involved in bombings and that sort of activity were just as puzzled by what was going on as the police. Well, if the bombings weren't political, they were part of a criminal conspiracy. I wasn't sure exactly what it was, but I had some ideas about who might be in it. And from something I overheard—with your stethoscope by the way—I knew that one phase of the plot was going to take place today."

"But you seemed to know that the paintings that were left were forgeries even before Wilson got there," said Lytell.

"I was fairly sure they were as soon as Gregory gave me the facts."

"As I recall," said Watson, "all he told you was that he was puzzled because the bomb squad wasn't from Scotland Yard."

"That was enough. After all, there had to be a reason for a fake squad to go to the auction rooms. And when I asked him about any missing artists and he told me that one had died in a suspicious fire, I had the answer. He must have been the artist who forged the paintings."

"I don't follow that," said Lytell.

"Whoever is behind this plot is not only a very clever but a completely ruthless man. He was not going to risk having the artist who forged the paintings give him away. So he had him killed."

Lytell stared at him.

"But this is appalling!" he said. "I was upset enough at losing the paintings. But if there's murder involved in it too . . ."

"It's a very complicated plot," said Holmes grimly. "And we're not at the end of it yet."

"But whoever is responsible must be apprehended! I trust you intend to continue on the case."

"I do."

"Well, if there's anything I can do to help . . ."

"As it happens, there is. Gregory isn't aware of all the ramifications of the crime as yet. He's treating it merely as an art theft—though a major one—and he'll notify dealers here and abroad, watch all known receivers of stolen property. But that will accomplish nothing. For, as I said, there's more to it than that."

"You also said that I could help. How?"

"I suspect that you'll be hearing from the thieves in a day or so."

"Hearing from them?"

"They will get in touch with you in one way or another, offer to give you back the pictures in exchange for a large sum of money. Part of their instructions will be that you say nothing about it to anyone—the police, me or anyone else. I suggest that you follow their instructions exactly."

"What? You're not serious!"

"I'm very serious."

"You mean, if I do hear from them I should not notify the police or you?"

"Absolutely not."

"I must say that's very strange advice coming from you, Holmes."

"Do you think I give it lightly?"

"I don't imagine you do anything lightly."

"You're quite right. I don't. As I said, there's much more involved here—and much more at stake—than you realize. Therefore I do not merely advise or suggest. I *urge* you to do exactly what you're told to do."

Lytell studied him intently for a moment. Then he nodded.

"You've made it clear that there are things you are not telling me," he said. "But if you trust someone, as I do you, you must trust that person completely. Very well, Holmes. I'll do as you say."

His hand on the bell pull, Andrew looked at Screamer.
"Why do you want to come up too?"

Screamer dropped her eyes, clutched at her skirt, and twisted the fold.

"Because I'm afraid to wait here alone."

"Afraid! You've never been afraid of anything in your life!"

"I have too!"

She had been strange ever since he had returned to the Wigginses' rooms that morning, reluctant to let him out of her sight even for a moment. It was only with the greatest difficulty that he could get her to leave the kitchen when he filled the tin tub and took the bath he needed so badly. Now she raised her eyes, looking at him shyly, imploringly, and he gave up.

"All right," he said and tugged at the bell pull.

The door was opened by a pleasant looking, middle-aged woman wearing an apron and a lace cap.

"Good afternoon," he said. "I'm Andrew Craigie. Mr. Holmes sent for me."

"Yes, he told me," she said. "It's the door at the top of the stairs."

He and Screamer went up the stairs. He knocked, and when Holmes said, "Come in," he opened the door.

Holmes was standing in front of the fireplace on the far side of the room; the heavyset man with the military mustache was sitting in an armchair to the left of it. A third man, wearing a tweed suit, stood near the door.

"Well, I'll be running along then, Holmes," he said. "I gather there's no point in my saying I'll keep in touch with you."

"No," said Holmes. "*I* will keep in touch with you."

The man's face cleared.

"I think I understand," he said. "Very well. Good-bye. Goodbye, Dr. Watson."

He left, and Holmes smiled at Andrew.

"I see you got my message," he said.

"Yes, sir. Sam gave it to me."

"And who's this?" asked Holmes, looking at Screamer.

"Sam's sister, Sara."

"Oh, yes. I've heard of her." He turned to the man in the armchair. "Watson, this is Andrew Craigie, whom I believe you've seen but never met. The young lady with him is Sam Wiggins's sister, better known as Screamer."

"How do you do?" said Watson, nodding gravely.

"Do you feel like undertaking another commission for me, Andrew?" asked Holmes.

"Of course, sir."

"Very well. I want you to go a boarding house at Twelve Henry Street in St. John's Wood and ask for a Mrs. John Harker. Tell her I've just returned to London and must see her immediately."

"Yes, sir."

"Time's very important, so take a hansom—here's ten bob—have him wait and bring her back here."

"Yes, sir." Then as Screamer tugged at his coat. "Is it all right if Screamer comes with me?"

"Quite all right. As a matter of fact, it's a good idea." He frowned. "One more thing. For reasons I can't go into, I'd rather Mrs. Harker didn't know who you are. So if she should ask you any questions, you had better be someone else."

"Who, sir?"

Holmes looked at Screamer. "What about Sam Wiggins?"

"Right, sir."

"You needn't come back up when you've brought Mrs. Harker here. And, Andrew . . ."

"Yes, sir."

"I haven't forgotten that we still have some unfinished business. I'll see you, and we'll take care of it in a day or so."

"Yes, sir?"

With Screamer trotting beside him, he left and hurried down the stairs.

"A hansom!" she said when they were outside. "Coo! I've never been in one in my life."

"I have," he said. "It's jam!"

He let a four-wheeler go by, waved to a hansom that was close behind it.

"What's up, young 'un?" said the cabby, stopping.

"Twelve Henry Street in St. John's Wood," said Andrew. "And we're in a hurry."

The cabby stared at him.

"Is this a cod?" he asked.

"If you're worried about the money . . . Here," he said, and he held up the ten-shilling note Holmes had given him.

The cabby looked at it, at him, then grinned.

"All right, guv'ner," he said, pulling the lever that opened the leather half-door. "In you get."

They climbed in. The cabby closed the door, slapped the reins on the horse's back, and they were off, rocking a little but moving swiftly and smoothly north. It took about ten minutes to get to the address, a large and respectable house with a white door.

"We'll only be a few minutes and then we'll want to go back," said Andrew, getting out. "Will you wait?"

"Sure, guv'ner," said the cabby, smiling. "Take your time."

It took more than a few minutes because, unlike Mrs. Hudson, the landlady here was not accustomed to having boys in ragged, badly fitting clothes knock at her door, and Andrew had some difficulty in persuading her to get Mrs. Harker for him. She was, when she finally appeared, an attractive, dark-haired woman with troubled blue eyes. Andrew gave her Holmes's message, and her pale, drawn face became even paler.

"He wants me to come there now?"

"Yes, ma'am. I have a hansom waiting."

She hesitated and, for a moment, Andrew thought

she was going to refuse. But finally she said, "Very well. Let me get my things."

When she came down the stairs again, she was wearing a hat and dark jacket and carrying a purse and her gloves. Andrew helped her into the hansom, told the cabby to take them back to Baker Street, and got in himself.

Sitting on the far side of the hansom, Mrs. Harker stared straight ahead of her. It was obvious that she was not only troubled but anxious, for she kept pulling at her gloves, first loosening them, then drawing them tighter. It seemed to Andrew that there was something familiar about her, but he couldn't tell what it was. Suddenly she turned, looked at him, at Screamer, then at him again.

"I'm sorry," she said. "I'm afraid I've been rather rude. Who are you?"

"Sam Wiggins, ma'am. This is my sister, Sara."

"How is it that Mr. Holmes sent you to get me?"

"I sometimes do things for him."

"Do things?"

"Run errands, carry messages."

"He does more than that," said Screamer. "He's one of the Baker Street Irregulars, and he helps Mr. Holmes on his cases."

"Does he?" Mrs. Harker smiled faintly. "You're very fond of your brother, aren't you?"

"Yes, ma'am. I am."

"It must be very exciting working with Mr. Holmes."

"It is," said Andrew. "He's not only the greatest detective in the world—he's a wonderful man."

"So I've heard. When did he get back from Paris?"

"I think . . . this morning."

"Oh." She looked at Andrew again. "How old are you, Sam?"

"Fourteen, ma'am."

"Fourteen." She sighed. "I don't know much about boys, but I would have thought you were older."

"No, ma'am."

"And where are you from?"

"Why, here. London."

"Are you? Somehow you don't sound like a Londoner. At least . . ." She glanced at Screamer.

"He's been to school a lot more than me," said Screamer. "That's why he talks better than me."

"I see. Well . . ."

The hansom drew up in front of 221B. Andrew helped Screamer and Mrs. Harker out and started to hand the cabby the ten shillings.

"No, no," said Mrs. Harker. "I'll pay for it."

"But Mr. Holmes gave me the money for it."

"It doesn't matter. I insist."

She paid the driver, and he touched his hat and drove off.

Mrs. Harker stood there for a moment, pulling nervously at her gloves again, then said, "Thank you very much for coming to get me, children," and went in.

Holmes opened the door for her himself.

"Come in, Mrs. Harker," he said.

"Thank you, Mr. Holmes. I understand you just got back from Paris this morning."

"That's correct."

"And . . . do you have any word for me?"

"I think so. I believe I've found your husband and your daughter."

She started. "You have?"

"Yes. As you suspected, they're no longer at the Claridge. However, I did find an American and his young daughter at a hotel on the Left Bank where they've been for about a week. They seem to fit the descriptions you gave me, but since the man is using a different name and I must be certain that the child is your daughter before I take any further steps, I suggest that you come to Paris with me tomorrow and identify them."

"Tomorrow?"

"Yes."

"But . . . but I can't do that."

"Why not?"

"It's such short notice."

"If I'm prepared to go when I've just returned, I should think you would be also."

"I am. It's just . . ."

"Mrs. Harker," said Holmes sternly, "do you want your child back or not?"

Her eyes filled with tears. "There's nothing . . . nothing in the world . . . I want more!"

"Then . . . ?"

"Very well. I'll go."

"Good. We'll take the noon train from Victoria station. I'll meet you there."

When Holmes had seen her out, he sat down opposite Watson and raised a quizzical eyebrow.

"You seem even more puzzled now than you were before, Watson," he said.

"I confess I am. You claimed you were in Paris when you weren't there, talked of people you could not have seen. And now you seem actually going there with Mrs. Harker, about whom—and about whose case—you expressed serious misgivings."

"Admirably put. Everything you say is true, Watson."

"And you still do not feel like explaining?"

"Not yet. I can only tell you what I told Lytell. That we are playing for very high stakes in a devious and complicated game. Therefore I must be devious also."

"I see. Well, I hope you know what you're doing."

"Amen to that. But," as Watson rose and went to the window, "at the moment I'm interested in what Mrs. Harker is doing. Can you see her?"

"Yes," said Watson. "She's just left the house and is walking north."

"And now is she crossing Baker Street and going into the telegraph office?"

"Yes, she is."

"Good." Holmes took out his watch. "Ten of six. We should still be able to catch him. Would you care to come out for a short stroll with me, Watson?"

"Why, yes. Where to?"

"To Jonathan Walker's shop."

Walker's languid assistant was just beginning to put out the lights when Holmes and Watson reached the shop. He said something over his shoulder, and Walker came out of his office and opened the door.

"Good evening, Mr. Holmes, Dr. Watson. Come in."

"I'm afraid we're rather late," said Holmes. "Weren't you closing up?"

"We needn't close on the dot of six. You were away, weren't you?"

"Yes. In Paris. I just got back this morning."

"That's a bit sooner than you thought. I trust your trip was successful."

"Not very. I saw your friend, Hassler, and he didn't have the Bruch concerto but promised to hunt for it for me. As for my case, I had to return here to get some more information, and I'll be going back to Paris again tomorrow."

"Tomorrow? Well, I hope that this time you accomplish what you set out to do."

"So do I. The reason I stopped by—and I apologize for trespassing on your good nature—was to ask your opinion about this." And he took a small package out of his pocket and gave it to Walker.

Walker unwrapped it and held it up to the light.

"A Fabergé snuff box," he said. "And an extremely nice one."

"It *is* Fabergé?"

"There's no question about it. Where did you get it?"

"In a little shop off Rue de Seine. They had three of them. I bought one and thought—if you were sure it was authentic—that when I got back there I'd buy the other two."

"It's certainly authentic. If you paid less than ten pounds for it, you did well."

"I paid considerably less than that."

"Then I congratulate you. If you do buy the other two and want to dispose of one or both of them, I'd be happy to buy them from you."

"I might very well consider that," said Holmes, taking back the snuff box. "Thank you very much. I hope you didn't mind my consulting you this way."

"Not at all. I was delighted to be of help. You're definitely leaving tomorrow?"

"Yes. On the noon train to Dover."

"Well, I hope you have a pleasant trip. In any case," he looked out the window at the fog that was beginning to dim the street lights, "you'll be lucky to be away for the next few days. I suspect we're in for a London particular."

13

Footsteps in the Fog

Walker was right. During the night the fog settled down on the city like a pall. As it mixed with the smoke from the factories and the thousands of coal fires in private homes, it became the special kind of fog known as a London particular; so dense, yellow, and impenetrable that it slowed traffic to a crawl and so acrid that it made the eyes smart.

Andrew and Screamer had gone to Madame Tussaud's Waxwork Museum early in the afternoon and had spent several hours there. Screamer had taken Andrew's hand in the Chamber of Horrors, frightened but fascinated as he explained how the guillotine worked and why Charlotte Corday was stabbing Marat in his bath. Walking slowly through the enormous, mirrored rooms, staring at the effigies of the great and near-great, they had forgotten the world outside, and it was only when they prepared to leave that they realized they could barely see Marylebone Road through the glass panels of the doors.

Screamer looked back at the nearest of the rooms where the queen and Albert stood, lifelike but forever still, surrounded by their children and said, "Do we have to go?"

"It's late, and it's going to take a while to walk home," said Andrew.

"Mum won't care. Not if I'm with you. But all right."

They pushed open the door, went out into the fog, and moved cautiously to the nearest traffic island. The gaslights in the iron standards had been lit, but they only glowed faintly, high overhead like dim, sick moons. Since Andrew and Screamer could not see more than six or eight feet through the murk, they listened intently before they hurried across the street. Then, hugging the buildings, they went west toward Baker Street. As they reached the corner, they heard the slow clop of hoofs, and a hansom came up Baker Street, turned into Marlebone Road, and stopped. A man carrying a bag got out and paid the driver. The hansom moved off again, and the man put down the bag and remained standing there; a tall man wearing a soft felt hat and a long travelling coat.

"What is it?" asked Screamer as Andrew stared at him.

He did not answer but moved closer to the corner, peering through the fog. He suddenly realized it was the fair man in the tweed suit they had seen in Holmes's rooms the day before.

Screamer recognized him at the same time.

"Isn't that . . . ?"

"Yes, the man who was leaving when we got to Mr. Holmes's."

"So he's going somewhere," she whispered. "What of it?"

"Travelling, you mean?"

"Yes."

"Then why did he get out of the hansom? Why is he standing there?"

"I dunno."

"Let's wait a minute and see."

"All right."

She moved closer to him, and they stood there, watching the dimly seen figure. The man paced up and down, looking down Baker Street and up Marylebone Road but never moving far from the bag. Again there was the sound of hoofs, and the man picked up the bag and moved to the curb. A four-wheeler came down Marylebone Road and, seeing him, the cabby drew up.

"Cab, sir?"

The man shook his head and, shrugging, the driver clucked to his horse and went on. Andrew frowned. There was something odd about the whole thing; not merely the fact that the man had gotten out of a hansom when he apparently still wanted a cab, but something else. And suddenly he realized what it was. The man had not been looking at the cabby when he shook his head but down at the horse's hoofs.

"I'm getting cold," said Screamer.

"I know. But something funny's going on."

"What?"

He pressed her hand in warning as another four-wheeler came up Baker Street, turned right into Marylebone Road and stopped. Again the man stepped forward, looking down. Then he picked up the bag and moved toward the growler. Andrew edged around the corner, peering down also. This horse had a white bandage wrapped around its right front fetlock. The driver, billycock hat tipped forward, face wrapped in a scarf, sat there stolidly, looking straight ahead. He said nothing to the man, and the man said nothing to him. He just opened the door of the four-wheeler and got in. It was only when the door closed that the driver turned his head slightly—and when he did, Andrew gasped. It was the cabby with the broken nose.

"Now what?" asked Screamer.

"That's the cabby I told you about. The one who took Mr. Dennison away and chased me." Then, as the cabby shook the reins and the growler moved off, "Look, you go home. I'll meet you there later."

"Where are you going?"

"I'm going to follow him."

"Why?"

"Because the man with the bag is a friend of Mr. Holmes. I want to see where the cabby's taking him."

"I'm coming too."

"Screamer, please . . ." The growler had disappeared into the fog. He could still hear the sound of the horse's hoofs, but in another minute it might be gone. "All right. On one condition. That you do just what I say. Will you?"

"Yes."

Hand in hand they went around the corner, hurrying along Marylebone Road after the four-wheeler. Now, for the first time, Andrew was thankful for the fog. It not only hid their movements but kept the growler to a walking pace so that they were able to catch it and keep up with it. The driver had not lit his lamps but they could make out the square, swaying shape as it rolled slowly through the thick, yellow obscurity. After a few minutes the growler turned right.

"Where are we?" asked Andrew.

Screamer squinted, trying to identify some landmark through the fog.

"I think . . . Portland Place."

They turned right also, walking close to the curb on the opposite side of the street from the growler. There was almost no one about, though once they nearly bumped into a man who loomed up suddenly out of the misty darkness. And when they went past the Hotel Langham where they had watched the actress Verna Tillett arrive, they saw a hansom waiting at the cab rank, the driver hunched disconsolately in his box.

On they went, the cold dampness of the fog chilling them, its foul taste in their mouths. The growler crossed Oxford Street, turned east and went by Hengler's Circus on Great Marlborough Street. They were now on the same side of the street as the growler, walking about twenty feet behind it. The fog muffled all sounds, making their footsteps almost inaudible, but even so, the cabby turned his head occasionally, looking back and seeming to listen and, when he did, they stopped and then went on again.

They went through Soho, around Soho Square, and came out into St. Giles Circus. Now the four-wheeler went north, and when it turned into Great Russell Street, Andrew suddenly knew where it was going. He touched Screamer's arm, leaned close to her.

"Be very quiet, very careful now," he whispered.

She nodded. As he had expected, the growler turned right, going south. About a hundred yards down the narrow street was the alley that led to the abandoned warehouse in which Holmes had been so interested.

Keeping his hand on Screamer's arm, Andrew went more slowly, expecting the growler to stop. But, though it slowed up also, it did not. Then, when it was a short distance past the entrance to the alley, a man stepped out of a doorway, waved to the cabby, and then retreated to the doorway again. The cabby waved back, and the four-wheeler went on, turning right on New Oxford Street.

Andrew stopped dead, thinking hard. He was still convinced that the growler's destination was the old warehouse. But if it was, why had it gone on? There could only be one reason. Someone wanted to make sure that it wasn't being followed. The cabby would make a circuit, going round by way of St. Giles Circus and then returning again. In the meantime, the man in the doorway would be watching to see if anyone was following. It would take at least five minutes for the growler to go round and come back again. And, since it was unlikely that there was anyone else in the warehouse—Holmes and Andrew had only seen Broken Nose and the well-dressed young man go in there—this would give Andrew a chance to do something that Holmes had not been able to do; go in and look around.

He leaned close to Screamer again and whispered, "You said if I let you come with me you'd do just what I told you to do."

She nodded.

"All right. Then go back to Baker Street and tell Mr. Holmes what happened. That the cabby he and I followed to the old warehouse picked up the man who was in his rooms yesterday and is taking him to the warehouse."

"What are you going to do?" she asked.

"I'm going in there for a minute to look around, then I'll come out here again and wait."

"No!" she said. "You can't. . . ."

"It's important!" he said angrily. "And you promised! Now go ahead!" And he turned her around and pushed her.

She looked at him over her shoulder, her eyes wide and frightened, then went pattering off toward Great Russell Street.

His heart thumping unevenly, Andrew peered through the fog. The man—and he was convinced it was the young, well-dressed man that he and Holmes had followed from the gin shop—was still in the doorway on the far side of the alley.

Andrew moved quickly but quietly to the mouth of the alley and went down it to the door of the warehouse. He tried the knob. The door was not locked. He pushed it open and went in. He found himself in a long, narrow corridor, dimly lit at its far end. A faint light also showed under a door to the left. He started down the corridor, then paused. Someone behind the closed door had groaned. Bending down, he looked through the keyhole.

From what he could see, the room was small and had probably been the warehouse office. A candle burned on a plain wooden table, and on the far side of the room was a cot. That was all he saw at first. Then he heard another groan and twisting sideways and looking to his left, he stiffened. There, handcuffed to a chair, was Mr. Dennison!

Andrew straightened up. Then, without thinking, he opened the door. Hearing it open, Dennison turned and stared at him. His hair was unkempt, he was unshaven and his face was thin and pale.

"Andrew!" he croaked. Then frowning uncertainly at Andrew's cropped head and badly fitting clothes, "Is it you?"

Andrew nodded.

"What are you doing here? How did you get here?"

"I followed a cabby. The one who took you away that night."

"Oh." The look of bewilderment remained, but a

faint light appeared in his lacklustre eyes. "I behaved very badly toward you—I know that now—and what I wanted to do was even worse, but . . . will you help me?"

Mutely, Andrew nodded again.

"Then go and get a policeman—go quickly!—and bring him back here."

As Andrew turned, the outside door opened, there were quick, light footsteps along the corridor, and Screamer came into the room.

"Screamer!" he said. "I told you . . ."

"I know. And I started to go. But when I got to the corner I remembered something Sam said this morning. Mr. Holmes ain't here. He's gone to Paris."

14

The Man in the Dark

Andrew stared at her. He had been out, doing some marketing for Mrs. Wiggins when Sam had come back from Baker Street. But if Screamer said Holmes was away, he was.

"Holmes?" said Dennison. "What's he got to do with this?"

Before Andrew could answer, there were footsteps on the cobbles of the alley outside.

"They're coming!" groaned Dennison. "Shut the door!"

Screamer, who was closest to it, pushed it closed.

Dennison looked around frantically. Except for the cot, the table and the chair to which he was handcuffed, the room was bare.

"The cot!" he said. "Hide under the cot. And if by some miracle you get away, call the police!"

Pushing Screamer ahead of him, Andrew ran across the room, and they both crawled under the cot. Reaching out, Andrew pulled down the blanket so that it hung over the edge of the cot, concealing them.

The warehouse door opened. There were footsteps in the corridor. They paused opposite the door, then went on again. Nearer at hand there was a dragging, scraping sound and, peering around the edge of the blanket, Andrew saw that Dennison was pushing the chair across the room so that it was as far from the cot as possible.

The outside door opened again. There were more footsteps in the corridor, and now the door of the small room opened.

"All right, Barney," said a voice. "Take the bracelets off him."

Again Andrew looked around the edge of the blanket. The slim, well-dressed young man from the gin shop stood in the doorway, a revolver in his hand. With him was the broken-nosed cabby. The cabby went over to Dennison, took out a key and unlocked the handcuffs, then lifted him to his feet.

"This way, Mr. Dennison," said the young man. Then, as he swayed unsteadily, "Having trouble walking?" He clicked his tongue in mock sympathy. "Help him, Barney."

Taking him by the arm, the cabby led him to the door. Gun ready, the young man watched him. Then the three of them disappeared up the corridor that led toward the interior of the warehouse.

Screamer, lying next to the wall, pulled at Andrew's jacket, and he crawled out from under the cot and helped her out. They tiptoed to the door. Andrew looked down the corridor. There was no sign of Dennison or the two men.

Again Screamer pulled at his jacket, nodding toward the outside door. Dennison had told them to escape if they could and get the police. Andrew had never been particularly fond of Dennison, but he had saved them just now and Andrew had a feeling that if anything was going to happen to him, it would happen before the police got there.

He leaned close to Screamer, whispered, "You go get the police. I'm going in there."

"No!"

"Yes!" he said, trying to push her toward the door. He felt her brace herself, resisting, knew there was no time to argue with her and gave up. He started down the corridor toward the interior of the warehouse with Screamer following close behind him.

At the end of the corridor was a large crate, and he got behind it, peering around its edge. The interior of the warehouse was enormous, cavernous. On a barrel in the center of it was an oil lamp. And standing in the circle of light that surrounded the lamp, bag in hand, was the man they had seen in Holmes's room and followed there.

"Do you have the money, Lytell?" asked a voice from somewhere in the darkness. It was not the voice of the slim young man. It was another voice, cultivated and authoritative.

Lytell nodded and held up the bag.

"Go get it, Barney," said the voice from the darkness.

Barney advanced into the lamp light, took the bag and opened it.

"All cummifo?"

"Seems to be," said Barney.

"Very good."

"What about the paintings?" asked Lytell.

"Ah, yes. The paintings. There's something I must do before we get to them. Sebastian, we're ready for Mr. Dennison now."

Sebastian, the slim, well dressed young man, appeared out of the darkness. He was holding Dennison's arm with one hand. In the other was the revolver.

"Dennison, I have you covered," said the voice. "A false move, and you're a dead man. Do you understand?"

Shaking, his drawn and unshaven face paler than ever, Dennison nodded.

"Good. Sebastian, give him your barker."

Releasing Dennison but standing close to him and watching him carefully, Sebastian handed him the revolver. Dennison looked down at it, then started to turn around.

"No," said the voice from the darkness. "Don't turn around. You see the man in front of you?"

Dennison nodded.

"His name is Adam Lytell. You will now shoot him."

"What?" Dennison stiffened. "No!"

He tried to drop the gun, but Barney was at his right side now and clutched his hand, holding his fingers around the butt of the revolver.

139

"Perhaps you'd better help him, Barney."

Spreading his legs and holding Dennison's right hand in both of his, Barney began forcing it upward. Dennison struggled, twisted and pulled, but Sebastian had him by the left arm, and he was no match for the two men.

Lytell had not moved. Though the color had left his face, he stood there calmly, his eyes on Dennison. Barney had forced Dennison's hand up so that the revolver was now pointing at Lytell's chest. Then, as he slipped his finger through the guard, prepared to pull the trigger, Screamer screamed—screamed even more loudly, shrilly, and piercingly than she had before.

Andrew, standing next to her, jumped. Barney's hand jerked up, and the gun went off, the bullet missing Lytell and thudding into the distant wall. Then, as all of them—Lytell, Dennison, Sebastian and Barney—turned to stare at the crate, the outside door of the warehouse crashed open and running footsteps came down the corridor.

"Quick, Barney! Do him!" said the voice from the darkness.

With an oath, Barney tore the gun from Dennison's hand, brought it down on his head. As Dennison fell to the ground, he turned and raised the gun again. When they had hidden behind the crate, Andrew had noticed that someone had left a heavy china mug on it. Now, hardly aware of what he was doing, he picked it up and threw it as hard as he could. It struck Barney in the back of the head, and again the gun went off harmlessly.

Then three men with guns in their hands ran past Screamer and Andrew: Holmes, Watson, and a large, leonine man wearing a bowler.

"Don't move, anyone!" said Holmes sharply. "The warehouse is surrounded!"

A shot rang out from the darkness, the bullet passing so close to Holmes that he winced. Whirling, he fired back. There was a groan and a gun clattered to the floor.

"You'd better take care of him, Gregory," said Holmes. "He's the man you really want—the brains behind every major crime in London during the last year or so." Then, turning to Lytell, "Are you all right?"

"Just barely," said Lytell, forcing a smile. "If it hadn't been for someone who screamed and someone who threw a mug at our broken-nosed friend here . . ." He looked at Screamer and Andrew who had come out from behind the crate. "I seem to have seen these two young people before."

"Yes," said Holmes. "I'm not sure what they're doing here myself. We'll get to that—and the reason we were delayed—later on. But first . . ."

He broke off as Inspector Gregory returned to the circle of lamp light holding a tall man with a neatly trimmed beard by the arm. The man was clutching his right hand, which was bleeding.

"Lytell," said Holmes, "I don't believe you know Mr. Jonathan Walker, do you?"

"I don't believe I do," said Lytell.

"Look at him again more closely," said Holmes. Then as Lytell started, "Now do you recognize him?"

"Yes," said Lytell. "It's my brother, Roger!"

15

Explanation

"Thank you," said Lytell. "I could use one."

He watched as Holmes poured the whiskey, added a splash of soda from the gasogene and gave it to him. He waited till Holmes had fixed drinks for himself and Watson, then raised his glass.

"To you, Holmes," he said. "And to the extraordinary talents that brought me here safely."

"I probably shouldn't drink to that," said Holmes. "But I will."

They had come back to Baker Street after leaving the warehouse and were now sitting around a fire that was particularly welcome after the damp chill of the fog outside.

"I promised you an explanation," said Holmes, sipping his drink and then setting it down. "But first I'd like to apologize for our delay in breaking into the warehouse. As you probably gathered, I had alerted Gregory, had you watched, and was ready to move when you drew the money from the bank."

"I suspected as much," said Lytell. "And also that the fog had complicated things a bit."

"Not too much," said Holmes. "I knew about the warehouse and was fairly sure that's where you would be taken. I had foreseen that they would have someone waiting outside to make sure you would not be followed. But what I did not foresee was that they would lock the warehouse door when they went in after you. If I had, I would have provided myself with a key. But, as it was, I had to pick the lock, which took two or three minutes."

"A bad two or three minutes, I must confess," said Lytell. "But when did you guess that my brother was behind what happened?"

"I suspected it the first time you came here to see me. It was fairly clear to me that the reason you acted so strangely at the Empire Club was that you had been drugged."

"Drugged?"

"Yes. With peyote, a cactus button, which is a drug used by Mexican and American Indian medicine men to cause hallucinations."

"That's true," said Watson. "You mentioned it to me."

"But why?" asked Lytell.

"Surely that's obvious now," said Holmes. "You were the oldest son, the heir to the title and the estate. Your father already had serious reservations about you because of your politics. And your brother, Roger, evidently thought that if you acted sufficiently outrageously—even though he was not in good favor himself—your father would disinherit you, and the estate would come to him."

"That never occurred to me," said Lytell. "Certainly not that Roger was responsible—possibly because I thought he was in the United States."

"It was the only logical explanation," said Holmes. "And it prompted me to do some investigating. What do you know of your brother's activities after he was sent down from Oxford?"

"Very little. Mother died shortly after he was born, and there was just enough difference in our ages—four years—so that we were never close. I had left Harrow by the time he went there. And the same was true of Oxford. As a matter of fact, I was never sure why he was sent down."

"Your father was able to hush it up, but he was expelled for cheating at cards. And then what?"

"As far as I know, he went to the United States."

Holmes shook his head. "He was supposed to, but he did not go to the United States until about two years after that. He stayed in London and, since your father had cut his allowance to a bare minimum, he began a career of minor crime along with a man who had been involved with him, in the cheating scandal at Oxford: a man named Dennison."

"The man he wanted to shoot me?"

"Yes. As I said, their crimes were minor to begin with. When they attempted a major one—a robbery—they were caught. Dennison gave evidence against your brother and got off, but your brother went to jail for a year."

"How is it I never knew that?"

"Again your father used his influence to protect the family name. Your brother had been using an alias, and your father saw to it that he was tried and sent to jail under his assumed name."

"Then he never went to America at all?"

"Yes, he did. When he got out of jail I suspect he had a meeting with your father, promised to go to the United States and stay there if he were given a sizeable amount of money. Your father probably agreed. In any case, he went to New York, but he didn't remain there. He stayed long enough to grow a beard, dye his hair and generally change his appearance as much as he could. Then, having established an address in New York and having arranged for someone to receive and forward his mail, he returned to London as Jonathan Walker."

"Was this the address I sent the cable to, telling him I was planning to sell the pictures?"

"Probably. Where did you get it?"

"From father's solicitor after father died. For some time before that father had said he didn't know where to reach Roger."

"Knowing what he did about Roger, he was probably

145

trying to protect you, keep you from getting in touch with him."

"But why did he come back?"

"Because a cash settlement—and possibly a regular remittance—wasn't enough for him. He wanted much more than that. And, while he was in jail, he had worked out a means of getting it."

"While he was in jail?"

Holmes nodded. "While there he met a man named Jerry Wragge, a well known putter-up, or organizer, of criminal activities. He learned from Wragge that one of the key elements in organized crime was the fence, or receiver, of stolen property. He arranged with Wragge to take over this role. When he came back to London, he did precisely that. With the money he had gotten from your father and additional money he got from Wragge, he bought the warehouse and also opened his shop on Baker Street. Someone who does importing and exporting, dealing in all sorts of things, is of course in a very good position to dispose of stolen goods. One interesting aspect of all this is that, shortly after your brother returned to London, Wragge was murdered."

"Are you saying that Roger murdered him or had him murdered?" said Lytell.

"At this late date it would be difficult to prove, but I think it's likely. Wragge was an important figure in the London underworld, and Roger wanted no rivals. He was determined to be alone at the top of the heap, the Napoleon of crime."

"Did you know all this from the beginning?" asked Watson. "When we first went to Walker's shop?"

"No, Watson. I knew from things that Gregory told me and information I gathered myself that someone was organizing London's criminal activities very efficiently. I also knew that I was under constant surveillance. I recognized several beggars who suddenly appeared around here as crows, criminal lookouts or spies. I first began to suspect Walker—or Roger— when he tried to mislead me, and possibly provide himself with an alibi, by saying that he himself had been approached and asked to act as a fence."

"I wondered why you refused to look into his case," said Watson. "And I suppose that was the reason he opened his shop here on Baker Street."

"Exactly. Besides being able to keep track of my movements and activities, what better place could he find for his headquarters? Who would expect him to establish it under the very nose of the man most criminals feared more than anyone else?"

"So far it all seems fairly clear," said Lytell. "But while I know how he stole the paintings, I'm still not sure I understand *why* he did."

"Though he was well on his way to becoming London's criminal overlord, he was still interested in the Lowther estate. When his attempt to turn your father against you failed and your father died, he turned his attention to you. If he could get you out of the way he would inherit not only the estate but the title."

"In other words, he stole the paintings to use them as bait."

"Precisely. At the same time, an opportunity had arisen for him to pay off an old score. By coincidence, Dennison, the associate who had betrayed him, given evidence against him, came to London from Cornwall where he had been teaching school. Roger saw him, had him kidnapped and taken to the warehouse. As you know, he intended to have him kill you—after all, Dennison did have a criminal record—then he was going to have Dennison killed in such a way that it would look as if *you* had killed him in a struggle."

"I see," said Lytell. "Is there more?"

"Yes," said Holmes, "but nothing that directly concerns you."

"What about that girl and boy, Screamer and Andrew? With all due respects to you, Holmes, I would probably not be here now if it weren't for them. And though I thanked them, I want to do a great deal more than that for them."

"Ah, yes," said Holmes. "I'm expecting them here tomorrow at one o'clock. I have some unfinished business to take care of with them myself. But when that's concluded, I'll arrange for you to see them."

16

The Final Stroke

The landlady let them in and went up the stairs with them.

"Ah, there you are," said Holmes when he opened the door. "Have you had lunch?"

"Yes, sir," said Andrew.

"Too bad. We were just going to have ours, and you could have had it with us." He looked thoughtfully at Screamer. "Sara . . . or do you prefer Screamer?"

"I don't care. I'm used to Screamer."

"Then, Screamer, I have a favor to ask of you. There's something I want Andrew to do. Would you mind waiting downstairs with Mrs. Hudson for a while?"

She moved closer to Andrew, clutching his sleeve.

"Will he have to go away again, the way he did that other time?"

"No, no. He won't leave this room."

"Well, why can't I stay too?"

"It would just be better if you didn't."

"Do you like trifle?" asked Mrs. Hudson.

"I don't think I ever had any," said Screamer.

"I've made some for the gentlemen's lunch. Come along with me and try it."

"All right," said Screamer and with a last look at Andrew, she went off.

"You know Dr. Watson, don't you?" said Holmes.

"Yes, I do. Good afternoon, sir."

"Hello, Andrew," said Watson.

"You look different today, Andrew," said Holmes.

"Is that a new jacket?"

"Yes, sir. Screamer took me to the Samaritan Society, and they gave it to me."

"It fits you better than your old one. In fact, it looks quite good. Now, Andrew, there are two things I want you to do. The first is quite simple. The second may be a bit more difficult." He led him to a desk that faced a window looking out onto a garden. "Here are some scrapbooks, all indexed alphabetically. And here is a pile of newspaper cuttings all dealing with people of one sort or another. I'd like you to go through the cuttings and paste them in their proper place in the scrapbooks."

"According to name, sir?"

"Yes. This one, for instance, about Moulton, the axe murderer, goes under 'M.' Clear?"

"Yes, sir."

"The next part of what I want you to do will, as I said, be a bit more difficult. I'm expecting someone here in a little while—someone whom, as it happens, you know. This person and I will talk—and the talk will probably become quite dramatic and emotional. I have no objection to your listening. In fact, I don't see how you can avoid it. But under no circumstances, no matter what is said, do I want you to react—to show in any way that it is of any interest to you. Is that clear?"

"Yes, sir."

"And you feel I can trust you to do exactly what I ask?"

"Yes, sir."

"Good."

"It may make it a little easier for you, Andrew," said Watson, "if I told you I've no idea what he's about myself. You see, he does like his little mysteries."

"My wonders to perform? I must confess I do," said Holmes. Then, at a light tap at the door, "Ah, lunch. Come in, Mrs. Hudson."

"I thought you'd like to know," said Mrs. Hudson, entering with a tray, "that Screamer *does* like trifle. In fact, she thinks it's jammy."

"I'm delighted to hear it," said Holmes. "Though I confess it sounds a bit redundant. You're sure you won't have anything, Andrew?"

"Yes, sir."

He had begun pasting the newspaper cuttings in the scrapbook and was finding them very interesting. Most of them dealt with crimes—murder, robbery, or forgery—but not all of them. Some were concerned with missing persons and others with people who had curious professions or interests: a man in Dorset who was trying to develop a stingless bee, for instance, and another near Salisbury who was building a flying machine with wings that flapped like a bird's.

Holmes and Watson had finished their lunch, and Andrew was reading an article about a woman who kept snakes in the attic of her house in Hampstead, when the downstairs door opened and closed. There were raised voices—that of a woman and that of Mrs. Hudson, who seemed to be protesting—then quick footsteps came up the stairs.

"This," said Holmes, "should be the person I'm expecting."

The door opened without a knock, and Mrs. Harker entered, her face flushed and her eyes bright with anger.

"Good afternoon, Mrs. Harker," said Holmes. "You seem a bit upset."

"That," she said, "is a decided understatement! I do not like having games played with me, Mr. Holmes!"

"Games?"

"What else would you call what happened? I agree to go to Paris with you, and we travel together to Dover where we board the Channel packet. Then you disappear—and it is only after the boat has sailed that I discover you are not aboard and there is no way I can return to London or even England until this morning!"

"I regret that," said Holmes. "Particularly regret that you had to spend the night in Calais. But it was necessary for someone to believe that I had in fact gone to Paris with you. On the other hand," and his voice became colder, firmer, "haven't you been playing games with me?"

"What? What do you mean?"

"You know very well what I mean. You have been trying to deceive me from the time you first came here. Your name is not Harker. You are not an American, and the case you begged me to look into for you was a complete fabrication."

The color left Mrs. Harker's cheeks.

"That's not true," she said. "At least, it's not completely true."

"Ah? Perhaps you'd better tell me what was true and what was not."

"Well, it's true that I'm not an American—though I've been there for the past ten years. And it's true that my name is not Harker. I'd rather not tell you what my real one is."

"Then suppose I tell you," said Holmes. "You are really Verna Tillett, the actress, who was supposed to open at the Adelphi last week, but for good reasons did not."

She stared at him.

"How did you know that?"

"Deduction and investigation. You made a slip when you first came here that convinced me you were—not only English—but a Londoner. The rest was merely a matter of deciding who you actually were."

"Then there's no need for me to continue to wear this," she said, pulling off a dark wig and shaking out the tawny hair Andrew remembered from the time he and Screamer had seen her arriving at the Hotel Langham.

"None. Though you were quite a convincing American," said Holmes. "But you still have not told me why you tried to deceive me."

"Because . . . because I had to," she said. "Because my child's life was at stake."

"Your child?"

"Yes. I said that not everything I told you was a lie.

152

That part was true. I do have a child but . . . I can't
. . . I don't dare tell you any more."

"Because you were told that if you did—if you went
to the police or told anyone about it—you would never
see your child again?"

"Yes."

"Miss Tillett, I am going to ask you a question I
have had to ask others before this. Do you trust me?"

She studied him, her blue eyes dark and troubled.

"I don't know. I think so."

"Then I can tell you that you no longer have anything to fear. If you will be completely open and honest
with me, I can—and will—return your child to you."

She stiffened, looking at him with a mixture of hope
and anxiety.

"How can you say that? How can you be sure . . . ?"

"I say it because I know things that you do not. The
man who threatened you, told you that you would not
see your child again if you did not do what he said, did
it for a specific purpose. To get me out of London."

"That's true. He told me what I was to say to you—
that story about my daughter in Paris—But I still don't
see how you can be sure . . ."

"I can because he was arrested last night and is now
in custody."

"Oh, no," she whispered. "Is that true—really true?"

"It is."

"Then . . . very well. I'll tell you anything you
want to know."

"Good. May I suggest that you sit down?" And he
drew up a chair for her.

"Thank you."

"Now begin at the beginning and tell us the whole
story."

"Oh." She hesitated. "It won't be easy. Parts of it are
very painful and . . ." She looked at Watson and Andrew.

"I'm sure they are. But I still think you should tell it.
You can rely on Watson's discretion and that of our
young friend here."

"Sam?" She smiled sadly at Andrew. "He's a little young for such a tale, but . . . I am, as you guessed, Verna Tillett. I was born in Lambeth, and my parents were street musicians. I began singing and dancing when I was quite small and—if I can be immodest—I was quite talented. By the time I was sixteen I was appearing in the music halls."

"I was not in London at the time," said Holmes, "but I believe I heard of you."

"When I was seventeen, I met a man. He was older than I was, the younger son of a good family, and we fell in love. He was reading law and had no money, but that did not matter. I was doing quite well in the music halls and told him I would support us both until he became a barrister. Though we did not tell his parents, we were going to be married. Then he died."

"Died?"

"Yes. It was very sudden, pneumonia. I was devastated. I had loved him very much. Then I discovered I was going to have a child."

"I see. What did you do?"

"I didn't know what to do. My father and mother were dead. I saw no point in telling Andrew's parents about it . . ."

"Andrew?"

"That was his name. And I wanted his child. There was a woman I was very close to, my dresser. No, she was much more than my dresser. She had been with me for two years and was my friend, my confidant. Her name was Agnes Craigie."

Andrew stirred, started to push back his chair, then became still as Holmes frowned at him.

"She was a Scot?"

"Yes. I was supposed to leave on a European tour—my first one. Agnes and I went to Bath, and I had the child there. A boy."

"Whom you named Andrew after his father?"

"Yes. Then we went south to a small fishing village in Cornwall, and I rented a house for Agnes. She was to say that the child was her brother's and keep him until I could come back for him."

"After which you left for your European tour."

"Yes. Agnes had been in the theatre for years before she came to me, and she persuaded me that I should. I had a contract, engagements, and she convinced me that it would be very bad for my career if I did not fulfill them. So I went."

"How long were you gone?"

"Two years. When I came back to London, I had begun to have an international reputation. I was offered engagements at the Tivoli and the Oxford and . . . well, I became afraid—afraid of what would happen if it became known that—though I had never been married—I had a child."

"So you continued to let Agnes take care of your son."

"Yes. I was still young—only twenty—and my career was very important to me. I sent Agnes money, went down to Cornwall to see the boy when I could. He was a wonderful boy, handsome, bright. Each time I saw him it was more difficult for me to leave him. Then I was offered an engagement in the United States. I was tempted to take him with me, but again Agnes persuaded me that it wasn't wise."

"So you went without him."

"Yes. I thought I would only be gone for about six months, possibly a year."

"How long were you gone?"

"Almost ten years."

"Ten years?"

She clasped her hands. "Please don't say it that way. I said that talking about it was difficult. I had been poor for so many years. Even when I was successful in the music halls, my life was uncertain. When I got to America, all that changed. After my first engagement, I was offered a dramatic part. I took it and began a new career as an actress. It was a completely different kind of life, and I revelled in it. There I was, a Cockney girl from Lambeth, being hailed, not for my singing and dancing, but for my acting. I didn't just play in New York. I toured as far west as San Francisco. Each time I went into a new play, I said, 'When this engagement is over, I'll go back to England. Or I'll have Agnes bring Andrew over here to me.' "

"But you didn't do either one."

"No. I sent her money, and she wrote me, told me what a fine boy Andrew was becoming. When he was about ten, I decided he should go to a good public school, and she found someone to tutor him, prepare him for it. Then she became ill and finally died. I was on tour at the time, didn't know it until I got back to New York."

"How did you find out about this?"

"The solicitors who had been taking care of my affairs—to whom I sent the money for Agnes and Andrew—wrote me and told me. They said the man who had been tutoring Andrew—a man named Dennison—had offered to look after him until I returned. I took the next boat back, went down to Cornwall . . . and found that Andrew and Dennison were gone!"

"This was just before you came to see me as Mrs. Harker?"

"Yes. I was desperate, consumed with guilt. If I had sent for Andrew and Agnes or come back before, it wouldn't have happened. I returned to London, went to see my solicitors . . . and that evening I got a message telling me that if I wanted word of my son I should be at the foot of Blackfriars Bridge at midnight."

"You went?"

"Of course. A four-wheeler pulled up. There was a man in it. He didn't get out and I never saw him, but he told me enough about Andrew and Agnes to convince me that he knew all about them and said that if I wanted Andrew back I must do exactly what he said."

"Which was to come to me with the story you did."

"Yes."

"I can fill in some background here. The man, Dennison, was not a particularly savory character. Though quite a good scholar, he had been sent down from Oxford, became involved in criminal activities here in London and then went into hiding in Cornwall. When he began tutoring Andrew, he sensed that there was something there that he could turn to his advantage."

"How?"

"Someone, he decided, was paying Agnes to keep Andrew there—someone with money. If he could find out who that person was—and what the story behind it was—he could probably blackmail that person. He tried questioning Agnes but got nowhere. However, when she became ill, she told him the names of your solicitors, Stroud and Dexter here on Baker Street, and he went to see them, offered to take care of Andrew until the absent parent, whom of course he didn't know, returned."

"But then why did he leave Cornwall? And where did he go?"

"He came here to London with Andrew. His plan was to keep him concealed, claim he had disappeared. This would enable him to find out who the missing parent was because, when he reported that Andrew was gone to the solicitors, they would undoubtedly bring him together with the father or the mother. Then he would either blackmail that person or—through some third party—claim that Andrew had been kidnapped and offer to return him for a large ransom."

"But he never did anything like that—never got in touch with me."

"He didn't have a chance to because his past caught up with him. Immediately after he got here—and before you arrived in England—he was seen by a man he had betrayed, a much cleverer and more dangerous man than Mr. Dennison. That man kidnapped him, found out what his plan was, and decided to use it for his own purposes."

"Was this the man in the four-wheeler? The man who made me come to you as Mrs. Harker?"

"It was."

"Then he has Andrew?"

"No. He tried to kidnap him as he had Dennison, but

Andrew got away. He's a very intelligent and resourceful boy. Nevertheless, knowing that you did not know where Andrew was, he pretended that he was keeping him prisoner."

"I'm not sure I understand this, but it's not important. The only thing that is important is Andrew. You said if I told you everything, you would help me find him."

"Yes, I did," said Holmes. "But there's something else that's even more important. How do you think Andrew is going to feel about you after what you've told me? After you left him alone for all these years?"

"Please!" she said, her eyes becoming misty. "Don't you think I've thought about that? Looking back now, I believe one of the reasons I didn't return before this was that I was afraid—afraid of what he might say. And when I did come back and discovered that he was gone, I thought I'd go mad. I know now that he means more to me than anyone or anything in the world, and I can only hope that if I explain, tell him what I've told you, he may understand and forgive me."

"Yes, I suppose he might," said Holmes slowly. He turned and looked at Andrew. "What do you say, Andrew?"

"Andrew?" She looked at Holmes and then at Andrew. "But he . . . he said his name was Sam. Sam Wiggins."

"I'm afraid I told him to say that, just as I told him to sit there quietly no matter what was said. But, though he did not know it until a few minutes ago, he is your son."

She became rigid. Her face, pale before, became even paler and her eyes widened and then became dark with anxiety.

"Andrew . . ." she whispered.

Andrew remained where he was. Once, swimming after a storm in Gorlyn, he had been caught by a huge wave and buffeted, tossed head over heels, drawn down into watery darkness and finally thrown breathless on the beach. He felt the same way now—so shaken by conflicting emotions that he dared not move. So much that he had not understood was clear now. So much that he had longed for was here within his reach. And yet the years of resentment and loneliness were still with him, too, bitter as salt in his mouth.

How did he feel about this woman who sat there with her eyes fixed on him? He did not know. Then suddenly, not with his brain—for thought has nothing to do with such matters—but with his whole body, he did know. The many things he felt became one, and he got to his feet and, moving awkwardly, went to her.

"Mother . . ." he said.

"Andrew . . . my darling boy!"

Then her tears came and, sobbing, she embraced him.

Watson cleared his throat.

"I think . . ." he began.

"So do I," said Holmes.

Rising, they took their hats and coats and went out.

"I must say, Holmes," said Watson when the door closed behind them, "I do think that was a little melodramatic."

"Do you? That's a strange remark for you to make after the drama you have always injected into your accounts of my cases."

"But that's a very different thing. In this instance . . ."

"I saw no point in forcing Miss Tillett to go through the whole painful story twice, so I arranged to have Andrew there when she first told it."

"Hmm. I must admit that it did work out well. Though I can't help wondering what will happen now."

"In what respect?"

"Well, as far as the Wigginses are concerned, for instance. It's clear that Andrew means a great deal to Screamer."

"And she to him. What will happen lies more in your province—that of the novelist—than mine. But I think I can predict that they will continue to see one another. When Andrew's mother hears the whole story of his adventures, I'm certain she will recognize the debt she owes Screamer and the Wigginses."

"I think you're probably right."

"I'm sure I am. Which leaves us with only one problem."

"What is that?"

"The fact that I *have* no problem, nothing to occupy my mind until another case comes along." He glanced at his companion. "May I ask what it is that you are humming?"

"If you were anything of a Savoyard, you would recognize it."

"I suspect you intend it to be the Policemen's chorus from *The Pirates of Penzance*."

"Exactly. And, with apologies to Mr. Gilbert, I was thinking . . . 'When constabulary duty has been done, has been done, a detective's life is not a happy one'."

"I have remarked before on what I suppose can be called your sense of humor, Watson. But I hope you are not under the illusion that humor and wit are the same thing."

ABOUT THE AUTHOR

ROBERT NEWMAN has written two novels for adults and many books for children including: *The Boy Who Could Fly, The Japanese, Merlin's Mistake, The Testing of Tertius, The Shattered Stone* and *Night Spell*.

He lives in a small village in Connecticut and is married to Dorothy Crayder, who is also a writer.

TEENAGERS FACE LIFE AND LOVE

Choose books filled with fun and adventure, discovery and disenchantment, failure and conquest, triumph and tragedy, life and love.

☐	13359	**THE LATE GREAT ME** Sandra Scoppettone	$1.95
☐	13691	**HOME BEFORE DARK** Sue Ellen Bridgers	$1.75
☐	13671	**ALL TOGETHER NOW** Sue Ellen Bridgers	$1.95
☐	12501	**PARDON ME, YOU'RE STEPPING ON MY EYEBALL!** Paul Zindel	$1.95
☐	11091	**A HOUSE FOR JONNIE O.** Blossom Elfman	$1.95
☐	14306	**ONE FAT SUMMER** Robert Lipsyte	$1.95
☐	13184	**I KNOW WHY THE CAGED BIRD SINGS** . Maya Angelou	$2.25
☐	12650	**QUEEN OF HEARTS** Bill & Vera Cleaver	$1.75
☐	12741	**MY DARLING, MY HAMBURGER** Paul Zindel	$1.95
☐	13555	**HEY DOLLFACE** Deborah Hautzig	$1.75
☐	13897	**WHERE THE RED FERN GROWS** Wilson Rawls	$2.25
☐ ☐	11829	**CONFESSIONS OF A TEENAGE BABOON** Paul Zindel	$1.95
☐	14730	**OUT OF LOVE** Hilma Wolitzer	$1.75
☐	14225	**SOMETHING FOR JOEY** Richard E. Peck	$2.25
☐	14687	**SUMMER OF MY GERMAN SOLDIER** Bette Greene	$2.25
☐	13693	**WINNING** Robin Brancato	$1.95
☐	13628	**IT'S NOT THE END OF THE WORLD** Judy Blume	$1.95

Buy them at your local bookstore or use this handy coupon for ordering:

Bantam Book Catalog

Here's your up-to-the-minute listing of over 1,400 titles by your favorite authors.

This illustrated, large format catalog gives a description of each title. For your convenience, it is divided into categories in fiction and non-fiction—gothics, science fiction, westerns, mysteries, cookbooks, mysticism and occult, biographies, history, family living, health, psychology, art.

So don't delay—take advantage of this special opportunity to increase your reading pleasure.

Just send us your name and address and 50¢ (to help defray postage and handling costs).